PAX

ALSO BY SARA PENNYPACKER

Summer of the Gypsy Moths
The Clementine series
The Amazing World of Stuart: Stuart's Cape
& Stuart Goes to School
Dumbstruck

SARA PENNYPACKER

PAX

ILLUSTRATED BY

JON KLASSEN

HarperCollins *Children's Books*

Author's note:
Fox communication is a complex system
of vocalization, gesture, scent, and expression.
The "dialogue" in italics in Pax's chapters attempts
to translate their eloquent language.

HarperCollins
PUBLISHERS
Since 1817

First published in hardback in Great Britain by HarperCollins *Children's Books* in 2016
First published in paperback in Great Britain by HarperCollins *Children's Books* in 2017

HarperCollins *Children's Books* is a division
of HarperCollins*Publishers* Ltd,

HarperCollins Publishers
1 London Bridge Street
London SE1 9GF

The HarperCollins *Children's Books* website address is
www.harpercollins.co.uk

1

PAX

ISBN 978-0-00-796874-9

Printed and bound by
CPI Group (UK) Ltd, Croydon, CR0 4YY

MIX
Paper from
responsible sources
FSC C007454

FSC™ is a non-profit international organisation established to promote
the responsible management of the world's forests. Products carrying the
FSC label are independently certified to assure consumers that they come
from forests that are managed to meet the social, economic and
ecological needs of present and future generations,
and other controlled sources.

Find out more about HarperCollins and the environment at
www.harpercollins.co.uk/green

To my agent, Steven Malk,
who said "Pax"

– S.P.

Just because it isn't happening here
doesn't mean it isn't happening.

———»———

*T*he fox felt the car slow before the boy did, as he felt everything first. Through the pads of his paws, along his spine, in the sensitive whiskers at his wrists. By the vibrations, he learned also that the road had grown coarser. He stretched up from his boy's lap and sniffed at threads of scent leaking in through the window, which told him they were now travelling into woodlands. The sharp odours of pine – wood, bark, cones, and needles – slivered through the air like blades, but beneath that, the fox recognised softer clover and wild garlic and ferns, and also a hundred things he had never encountered before but that smelled green and urgent.

The boy sensed something now, too. He pulled his pet back to him and gripped his baseball glove more tightly.

The boy's anxiety surprised the fox. The few times they had travelled in the car before, the boy had been calm or even excited. The fox nudged his muzzle into the glove's webbing, although he hated the leather smell. His boy always laughed when he did this. He would close the glove around his pet's head, play-wrestling, and in this way the fox would distract him.

But today the boy lifted his pet and buried his face in the fox's white ruff, pressing hard.

It was then that the fox realised his boy was crying. He twisted round to study his face to be sure. Yes, crying – although without a sound, something the fox had never known him to do. The boy hadn't shed tears for a very long time, but the fox remembered: always before he had cried out, as if to demand that attention be paid to the curious occurrence of salty water streaming from his eyes.

The fox licked at the tears and then grew more confused. There was no scent of blood. He squirmed out of the boy's arms to inspect his human more carefully, alarmed that he could have failed to notice an injury, although his sense of smell was never wrong. No, no blood; not even the under-skin pooling of a bruise or the marrow leak of a cracked bone, which had happened once.

The car pulled to the right, and the suitcase beside them shifted. By its scent, the fox knew it held the boy's clothing and the things from his room he handled most often: the photo he kept on top of his bureau and the items he hid in the bottom drawer. He pawed at a corner, hoping to pry the suitcase open enough for the boy's weak nose to smell these favoured things and be comforted. But just then the car slowed again, this time to a rumbling crawl. The boy slumped forward, his head in his hands.

The fox's heartbeat climbed and the brushy hairs of his tail lifted. The charred metal scent of the father's new clothing was burning his throat. He leaped to the window and scratched at it. Sometimes at home his boy would raise a similar glass wall if he did this. He always felt better when the glass wall was lifted.

Instead, the boy pulled him down on to his lap again and spoke to his father in a begging tone. The fox had learned the meaning of many human words, and he heard him use one of them now: "NO." Often the "no" word was linked to one of the two names he knew: his own and

3

his boy's. He listened carefully, but today it was just the "NO," pleaded to the father over and over.

The car juddered to a full stop and tilted off to the right, a cloud of dust rising beyond the window. The father reached over the seat again, and after saying something to his son in a soft voice that didn't match his hard lie-scent, he grasped the fox by the scruff of the neck.

His boy did not resist, so the fox did not resist. He hung limp and vulnerable in the man's grasp, although he was now frightened enough to nip. He would not displease his humans today. The father opened the car door and strode over gravel and patchy weeds to the edge of a wood. The boy got out and followed.

The father set the fox down, and the fox bounded out of his reach. He locked his gaze on his two humans, surprised to notice that they were nearly the same height now. The boy had grown very tall recently.

The father pointed to the woods. The boy looked at his father for a long moment, his eyes streaming again. And then he dried his face with the neck of his T-shirt and nodded. He reached into his jeans pocket and withdrew an old plastic soldier, the fox's favorite toy.

The fox came to alert, ready for the familiar game. His

boy would throw the toy, and he would track it down – a feat the boy always seemed to find remarkable. He would retrieve the toy and wait with it in his mouth until the boy found him and took it back to toss again.

And sure enough, the boy held the toy soldier aloft and then hurled it into the woods. The fox's relief – they were only here to play the game! – made him careless. He streaked toward the woods without looking back at his humans. If he had, he would have seen the boy wrench away from his father and cross his arms over his face, and he would have returned. Whatever his boy needed – protection, distraction, affection – he would have offered.

Instead, he set off after the toy. Finding it was slightly more difficult than usual, as there were so many other, fresher odours in the woods. But only slightly – after all, the scent of his boy was also on the toy. That scent he could find anywhere.

The toy soldier lay face down at the burled root of a butternut tree, as if he had pitched himself there in despair. His rifle, its butt pressed tirelessly against his face, was buried to the hilt in leaf litter. The fox nudged the toy free, took it between his teeth, and rose on his haunches to allow his boy to find him.

In the still woods, the only movements were bars of sunlight glinting like green glass through the leafy canopy. He stretched higher. There was no sign of his boy. A prickle of worry shivered up the fox's spine. He dropped the toy and barked. There was no response. He barked again, and again was answered by only silence. If this was a new game, he did not like it.

He picked up the toy soldier and began to retrace his trail. As he loped out of the woods, a jay streaked in above him, shrieking. The fox froze, torn.

His boy was waiting to play the game. But birds! Hours upon hours he had watched birds from his pen, quivering at the sight of them slicing the sky as recklessly as the lightning he often saw on summer evenings. The freedom of their flights always mesmerised him.

The jay called again, deeper in the forest now, but answered by a chorus of reply. For one more moment the fox hesitated, peering into the trees for another sight of the electric-blue wedge.

And then, behind him, he heard a car door slam shut, and then another. He bounded at full speed, heedless of the briars that tore at his cheeks. The car's engine roared to life, and the fox skidded to a stop at the edge of the road.

His boy rolled the window down and reached his arms out. And as the car sped away in a pelting spray of gravel, the father cried out the boy's name, *"Peter!"* And the boy cried out the only other name the fox knew.

"Pax!"

2

" *So there were lots of them.*"

Peter heard how stupid it sounded, but he couldn't help repeating it. "Lots." He plowed his fingers through the heap of plastic soldiers in the battered cookie tin – identical except for their poses: standing, kneeling, and prone, all with rifles pressed hard to their olive-green cheeks. "I always thought he just had the one."

"No. I was always stepping on them. He must have had hundreds. A whole army of them." The grandfather laughed at his own accidental joke, but Peter didn't. He turned his head and looked intently out the window, as if he had just caught sight of something in the darkening back yard. He raised a hand to draw his knuckles up his jaw line, exactly the way his father rasped his beard stubble, and wiped surreptitiously at the tears that had brimmed. What kind of a baby cried about something like this?

And why was he crying at all, anyway? He was twelve and he hadn't cried for years, not even when he'd fractured his thumb bare-handing Josh Hourihan's pop fly. That had hurt a lot, but he'd only cursed through the pain waiting with the coach for X-rays. Man up. But today, *twice*.

Peter lifted a soldier from the tin and drifted back to the day he'd found one just like it in his father's desk. "What's this?" he'd asked, holding it up.

Peter's father had reached over and taken it, his face softening. "Huh. Been a long time. That was my favourite toy when I was a kid."

"Can I have it?"

His dad had tossed the soldier back. "Sure."

Peter had stood it up on the windowsill beside his bed, pointing the little plastic rifle out in a satisfying show of defence. But within the hour Pax had swiped it, which made Peter laugh – just like him, Pax had to have it.

Peter dropped the toy back into the tin and was about

to snap the lid back on when he noticed the edge of a yellowed photo sticking up from the mound of soldiers.

He tugged it free. His dad, at maybe ten or eleven, with one arm draped around a dog. Looked like part-collie, part-a-hundred-other-things. Looked like a good dog, the kind you would tell your own son about. "I never knew Dad had a dog," he said, passing the photo to his grandfather.

"That's Duke. Dumbest creature ever born, always underfoot." The old man looked more closely at the picture, and then over at Peter as if seeing something for the first time. "You've got the same black hair as your dad." He rubbed at the fringe of grey fuzz banding the top of his head. "I had it too, way back. And look, he was scrawny then, too, same as you, same as me, with those ears like a jug. The men in our family – I guess our apples don't fall far from the tree, eh?"

"No, sir." Peter forced a small smile, but it didn't hold up. "Underfoot." That was the word Peter's father had used. "He can't have that fox underfoot. He doesn't move as fast as he used to. You stay out of the way, too. He's not used to having a kid around."

"You know, war came and I went and served, like my father. Like your father now. Duty calls, and we answer in this family. No, sir, our apples don't fall far from the tree." He handed back the photo. "Your father and that dog. They were inseparable. I'd almost forgotten."

Peter put the photo back into the tin and pressed the lid down tight, then slid it under the bed, where he'd found it. He looked out the window again. He couldn't risk talking about pets right now. He didn't want to hear about duty. And he sure didn't want to hear any more about apples and the trees they were stuck underneath. "What time does school start here?" he asked, not turning round.

"Eight. They said to show up early, introduce yourself to the homeroom teacher. Mrs. Mirez, or Ramirez . . . something. I got you some supplies." The old man nodded over to a spiral notebook, a beat-up thermos, and a bunch of stubby pencils bundled together with a thick rubber band.

Peter walked over to the desk and put everything into

11

his rucksack. "Thanks. Bus or walk?"

"Walk. Your father went to that school, and he walked. Follow Ash to the end, turn right on School Street, and you'll see it – big brick building. School Street – get it? You leave by seven thirty, you'll have plenty of time."

Peter nodded. He wanted to be left alone. "Okay. I'm all set. I guess I'll go to bed."

"Good," his grandfather replied, not bothering to hide the relief in his voice. He left, closing the door behind him firmly as if to say, *You can have this room, but the rest of the house is mine.*

Peter stood by the door and listened to him walk away. After a minute, he heard the sound of dishes clattering in the sink. He pictured his grandfather in the cramped kitchen where they'd eaten their silent dinner of stew, the kitchen that reeked so strongly of fried onions that Peter figured the smell would outlive his grandfather. After a hundred years of scrubbing by a dozen different families, this house would probably still smell bitter.

Peter heard his grandfather shuffle back along the hall to his bedroom, and then the low spark as the television caught, the volume turned down, an agitated news commentator barely audible. Only then did he toe off his

12

trainers and lie down on the narrow bed.

Six months – maybe more – of living here with his grandfather, who always seemed on the verge of blowing up. "What's he always so mad about, anyway?" Peter had asked his father once, years ago.

"Everything. Life," his father had answered. "He got worse after your grandmother died."

After his own mother had died, Peter had watched his father anxiously. At first, there had just been a frightening silence. But gradually his face had hardened into the permanent threat of a scowl, and his hands clenched in fists by his sides as if itching for something to set him off.

Peter learned to avoid being that something. Learned to stay out of his way.

The smell of stale grease and onions crawled over him, seeping from the walls, from the bed itself. He opened the window beside him.

The April breeze that blew in was chilly. Pax had never been alone outside before, except in his pen. Peter tried to extinguish the last sight he'd had of his fox. He probably hadn't followed their car for long. But the image of him flopping down on the gravel shoulder, confused, was worse.

13

Peter's anxiety began to stir. All day, the whole ride here, Peter had sensed it coiling. It always seemed like a snake to him, his anxiety – waiting just out of sight, ready to slither up his spine, hissing its familiar taunt. *You aren't where you should be. Something bad is going to happen because you aren't where you should be.*

He rolled over and pulled the cookie tin out from under the bed. He fished out the photo of his father with one arm slung so casually around the black-and-white dog. As if he had never worried he could lose him.

Inseparable. He hadn't missed the note of pride that had entered his grandfather's voice as he'd said that. Of course he'd been proud – he'd raised a son who knew about loyalty and responsibility. Who knew that a kid and his pet should be inseparable. Suddenly the word itself seemed an accusation. He and Pax, what were they then . . . separable?

They weren't, though. Sometimes, in fact, Peter had had the strange sensation that he and Pax merged. The first time it happened had been the first time he'd taken Pax outdoors. The kit had seen a bird and had strained against the leash, trembling as though electrified. And Peter had seen the bird through Pax's eyes – the miraculous

14

lightning flight, the impossible freedom and speed. He'd felt his own skin thrill in full-body shivers, and his own shoulders burn as though yearning for wings.

It had happened again this afternoon. He had felt the car spin away as though he were the one being left. His heart had quickened with panic.

Tears stung again, and Peter palmed them with frustrated swipes. His father had said it was the right thing to do. "War is coming. It means sacrifices for everybody. I have to serve – it's my duty. And you have to go away."

Of course, he'd been half expecting it. Two of his friends' families had already packed up and left when the evacuation rumours had begun. What he hadn't expected was the rest. The worst part. "And that fox . . . well, it's time to send him back to the wild anyway."

A coyote howled then, so nearby that it made Peter jump. A second one answered, and then a third. Peter sat up and slammed the window shut, but it was too late. The yips and howls, and what they meant, were in his head now.

Peter had only two bad memories of his mother. He had a lot of good ones, too, and he often took those out to comfort himself, although he worried that they might fade from so much exposure. But the two bad ones he'd buried deep. He did everything in his power to keep them buried. Now the coyotes were baying in his head, unearthing one of them.

When he'd been about five, he'd come upon his mother standing dismayed beside a bed of blood-red tulips. Half of them were standing at attention, half of them splayed over the ground, their blossoms crumpling.

"A rabbit got them. He must think the stems are delicious. The little devil."

Peter had helped his father set a trap that night. "We won't hurt him, right?"

"Fine. We'll just catch him, then drive him into the next town. Let him eat someone else's tulips."

Peter had baited the trap himself with a carrot, then begged his father to let him sleep in the garden to keep watch. His father had said no, but helped him set an alarm clock so he'd be the first to awaken. When it went off, Peter had run to his mother's room to lead her outside by the hand to see the surprise.

The trap lay on its side at the bottom of a

freshly scraped crater at least five feet across. Inside was a baby rabbit, dead. There wasn't a single mark on its little body, but the cage was scratched and dented, and the ground all around clawed to rubble.

"Coyotes," his father said, joining them. "They must have scared it to death trying to get in. And none of us even woke up."

Peter's mother had opened the trap and lifted out the lifeless form. She held it to her cheek. "They were just tulips. Only a few tulips."

Peter found the carrot, one end nibbled off, and threw it as far away as he could. Then his mother had placed the rabbit's body in his cupped palms and gone to get a shovel. With a single finger, Peter had traced its ears, unfurling like ferns from its face, and its paws, miraculously tiny, and the soft fur of

its neck, slick with his mother's tears.

When she'd returned, his mother had touched his face, which burned with shame. "It's okay. You didn't know."

But it wasn't okay. For a long time afterward, when Peter closed his eyes, he'd seen coyotes. Their claws raking dirt, their jaws snapping. He saw himself where he should have been: keeping watch in the garden that night. Over and over, he saw himself doing what he should have: rising from his sleeping bag, finding a rock, and hurling it. He saw the coyotes fleeing back into the darkness, and he saw himself opening the trap to set the rabbit free.

And with that memory, the anxiety snake struck so hard that it stunned Peter's breath out of him. He hadn't been where he should have been the night the coyotes killed the rabbit, and he wasn't where he should be now.

He gasped to fill his lungs and sat bolt upright. He tore the photo in half and then in half again and pitched the pieces under the bed.

Leaving Pax *hadn't* been the right thing to do.

He jumped to his feet – he'd already lost a lot of time. He fished some cargos, a long-sleeved camouflage T-shirt, and a fleece sweatshirt from his suitcase, and then an extra set of underwear and socks. He stuffed everything into his rucksack except the sweatshirt, which he tied around his waist. Jackknife in his jeans pocket. Wallet. He debated for a minute between his hiking boots and trainers and decided on the boots, although he didn't put them on.

He looked around the room, hoping to find a torch or anything resembling camping equipment. The room had been his father's when he'd been a boy, but aside from a few books on a shelf, it was clear his grandfather had cleaned all his things out. The cookie tin had seemed to surprise him – an oversight. Peter bumped his fingers over the spines of the books.

An atlas. He pulled it down, amazed at his luck, and flipped through it until he came to the map that showed the route he and his father had travelled. "You'll only be three hundred miles away." His father had tried to bridge the silence of the drive a couple of times. "I get a day off, I'll come." Peter had known that it would never happen. They didn't give days off in war.

Besides, it wasn't his father he was already missing.

And then he saw something he hadn't realised: the highway snaked around a long range of foothills. If he cut straight across those instead of following the highway, he could save a lot of time, plus reduce the risk of being caught. He started to rip out the page, then realised he couldn't leave his grandfather such an obvious clue. Instead, he studied the map for a long moment, then replaced the atlas on the shelf.

Three hundred miles. It looked like he could shave off a hundred of them by taking the shortcut, so say around two hundred. If he could walk at least thirty miles a day, he could make it in a week or less.

They'd left Pax at the head of the access road that led to the ruins of an old rope mill. Peter had insisted on this road because hardly anyone ever used it – Pax didn't know about traffic – and because there were woods and fields all around. He'd go back and find Pax there, waiting, in seven days. He wouldn't let himself think about what might happen to a tame fox in those seven days. No, Pax would be waiting at the side of the road, right where they'd left him. He'd be hungry, for sure, and probably scared, but he'd be okay. Peter would take him home. They would stay there. Just let someone try to make him leave this time. *That* was the right thing to do.

He and Pax. Inseparable.

He glanced around the room again, resisting the urge to just *run*. He couldn't afford to miss anything. The bed. He pulled the blanket off, rumpled the sheets, and punched the pillow until it looked slept on. From his suitcase he took out the picture of his mother he'd kept on his bureau – the one taken on her last birthday, holding up the kite Peter had made for her, and smiling as if she'd never had a better present in her life – and slid it into his rucksack.

Next, he pulled out the things of hers that he'd kept hidden in his bottom drawer at home. Her gardening gloves, still smudged with the last soil she'd ever lifted; a box of her favourite tea, which had long ago lost its peppermint scent; the thick candy-cane-striped kneesocks she wore in winter. He touched them all, wishing he could take everything back home where it belonged, and then chose the smallest of the items – a gold bracelet with an enameled phoenix charm she'd worn every day – and tucked it into the middle of his rucksack with the photo.

Peter surveyed the room a last time. He eyed his baseball and glove and then crossed to the bureau and stuffed them into the rucksack. They didn't weigh much, and he'd want them when he was back home. Besides, he just felt better when he had them. Then he eased the door open and crept to the kitchen.

He set the rucksack on the oak table, and in the dim light from above the stove, he began to pack supplies. A box of raisins, a sleeve of crackers, and a half-empty jar of peanut butter – Pax would come out of any hiding spot for peanut butter. From the refrigerator, he took a bunch of string cheese sticks and two oranges. He filled the thermos with water and then hunted through drawers until he found matches, which he wrapped in tinfoil. Under the sink he scored two lucky finds: a roll of duct tape and box of heavy-duty garbage bags. A tarp would have been better, but he took two bags with gratitude and zipped the pack.

Finally he took a sheet of paper from the pad beside the phone and began a note: DEAR GRANDFATHER. Peter looked at the words for a minute, as if they were a foreign language, and then crumpled the paper up and started a new note. I LEFT EARLY. WANTED TO GET A GOOD START ON SCHOOL. SEE YOU TONIGHT. He stared at that page for a while, too, wondering if it sounded as guilty as he felt. At last, he added, THANKS FOR EVERYTHING – PETER, placed the note under the saltshaker, and slipped out.

On the brick walk, he shrugged on his sweatshirt and crouched to lace his boots. He straightened up and shouldered his rucksack. Then he took a moment to look around. The house behind him looked smaller than it had when he'd arrived, as if it were already receding into the past. Across the street, clouds scudded along the horizon, and a half-moon suddenly emerged, brightening the road ahead.

3

*P*ax was hungry and cold, but what had woken him was the sense that he needed cover. He blinked and edged backward. What felt like the comforting bars of his pen gave way in brittle snaps. He turned to find the stand of dried milkweed stalks he'd wedged himself against a few hours before.

He barked for Peter and remembered: his boy was gone.

Pax wasn't used to being alone. He had been born into a squirming litter of four, but his father had disappeared before the kits had even learned his scent, and soon after that, his mother had failed to come home one morning.

One by one, his brothers and sister had died, leaving his the only heartbeat in the cold den until the boy, Peter, had lifted him out.

Since that time, whenever his boy was gone, Pax would pace his pen until Peter returned. And at night he always whined to come inside, where he could listen to his human's breathing.

Pax loved his boy, but more than that, he felt responsible for Peter, for protecting him. When he couldn't perform this role, he suffered.

Pax shook the night's rain off his back and headed for the road without even stretching his stiff muscles, straining for his boy's scent.

He couldn't find it – the night's winds had swept the ground clean of any trace. But among the hundreds of odours rising on the early morning breeze, he found something that reminded him of his boy: acorns. Peter had often scooped up handfuls and sprinkled them over Pax's back, laughing to see him shake them off and then crack them to get at the meat. The familiar scent seemed a promise to him now, and he trotted toward it.

The acorns were scattered around the base of a lightning-struck oak a few full-bounds north of where he had last seen his boy. He crunched at a few of them, but found only shrivelled, mouldy nubs inside. Then he settled himself on the fallen trunk, ears trained for any sound on the road.

While he waited, Pax licked his fur dry and clean, taking comfort in the lingering Peter-scent he found there. Then he turned his attention to his forepaws, painstakingly cleaning the many cuts in their pads.

Whenever he was anxious, Pax dug at the floor of his pen. He always shredded his paws on the rough concrete buried beneath, but he could not control the urge. In the week before, he'd dug nearly every day.

When his paws were cleaned, he curled them up under his chest to wait. The morning air pulsed with the noises of spring. The long night before, they had alarmed Pax. The blackness had quivered with the rustle of night prowlers, and even the sounds of the trees themselves – leaves unfurling, sap coursing up new wood, the tiny cracklings of expanding bark – had startled him over and over as he waited for Peter to return. Finally, as dawn had begun to silver the sky, he'd fallen into a shivering sleep.

Now, though, the same sounds called to him. A hundred times his sensitive ears pricked, and he almost sprang up to investigate. But each time, he remembered his boy and stilled himself. The humans had good memories, so they would come back to this spot. But they relied on sight alone – all their other senses being so weak – so if they did not see him when they returned, they might leave again. Pax would stay beside the road and ignore all temptations, including the strong urge he felt to head south, the direction his instinct told him would lead him back to his home. He would stay at this spot until his boy came for him.

Above him, a vulture cruised the thermals. A lazy hunter, it was searching for the lifeless shape of carrion. When it found the red-furred form of the fox, motionless but giving off no odour of decay, it circled lower to investigate.

Pax registered an instinctive alarm at the cool flicker of V-shaped shadow. He jumped from the trunk and scratched at the dirt beneath.

The ground seemed to answer with a distant rumble, like a growling heart. Pax stretched high, the danger from above forgotten. The last time he had seen his boy, there had been vibrations like this along this very road. He tore over the gravel shoulder to the exact spot where his humans had left him.

The vibrations grew to a roar. Pax rose on his haunches to be seen. But the source was not his boy's car. It was not a car at all. As it loomed up, it seemed to the fox to be as large as the house his humans lived in.

The truck was green. Not the growing green of the trees all around, but a dull olive, a colour death might wear when it claimed these trees. The same dull olive of the toy soldier the fox had cached in the milkweed stalks. It stank of diesel and the same charred metal scent that had clung to his boy's father's new clothing. In a cloud of dust and sprayed stones, the truck charged past, followed by another and another and another.

Pax bounded away from the road. The vulture soared up and away with a single beat of its wings.

4

*N*ot hunting for his grandfather's torch — that was the first mistake of the trip. The moon had lit Peter's way for maybe two hours before it had drowned beneath thick clouds. He'd stumbled along in the dark for another hour before giving up. He'd slit open the sides of a bin bag to make a long mat and cut the other to wear as a poncho against the cold mist, and slept beside a culvert, his baseball mitt for a pillow. Actually, "slept" was a wild overstatement, and when the first low sun rays stabbed his eyelids, he'd awakened cold and wet from whatever dozing he'd managed.

His first thoughts were of Pax – where was he this morning? Was he wet and cold, too? Was he afraid? "I'm coming," he said out loud as he rolled the bin bags back into his pack. "Hold on."

He ate a stick of cheese and a couple of crackers, slugged a long drink of water, then laced his boots and climbed up to the road.

He was stiff and sore, but at least his anxiety had relaxed its grip. He probably hadn't travelled much more than seven or eight miles, but there was still a whole day before his grandfather would get home from work and even suspect he was gone.

According to the atlas map, he probably had another twenty miles to go before hitting the highway. After that, he could turn west for the shortcut anywhere that looked promising. He'd sleep deep in woods tonight, out of civilisation, the riskiest part of the trip behind him.

He wished he'd paid more attention as he'd driven with his father the day before – mistake number two – but he only recalled there'd been a single sleepy town right after they'd exited the highway, and then stretches of woodlands broken only by occasional farms.

Peter walked for five full hours. Blisters formed on

his heels, and his shoulders ached from the rucksack. But every step brought him closer to Pax and the home he should never have left, and he felt hopeful. Until a little after noon, when he hit a cluster of buildings that passed for a town square.

Immediately, it seemed every person he passed was eyeing him suspiciously, wondering why he wasn't in the school he'd noticed a little while back. When a woman dragging a toddler stopped to stare outright, Peter pretended to study the window display in the hardware shop beside him.

In the glass, he saw his reflection, and the remnants of his hopeful mood melted. His hair was tangled with leaves, his sweatshirt streaked in mud, and his nose reddened with what promised to be a full-faced sunburn by the end of the day. The kid in the window looked like a runaway – one who hadn't prepared very well.

He sensed the woman moving on, but before he could leave, a shadow loomed over his shoulder.

"Need something, young man?"

Peter looked up. A man in a blue jacket emblazoned with the shop logo stood in the doorway, smoking. His arms were crossed over a sagging belly, and his hair was a thinning grey, but something about the way he was peering down his nose reminded Peter of a hawk he'd once seen searching for prey from the top of a cedar. He pointed to the window.

Peter looked back at the display – seed packets and gardening tools. "Oh, no, I was just . . . uh, do you sell torches?"

The man cocked his head and eyed Peter while he took a drag on his cigarette, and again Peter was reminded of the hawk. Finally he nodded. "Aisle seven. No school today?"

"Lunch break. Got to hurry back."

The man stubbed out his cigarette and followed him inside, hovering nearby while Peter chose the cheapest torch on the rack and a pack of double As, and even shadowed him as he checked out.

Outside, Peter let out the breath he hadn't known he'd been holding. He wedged everything into his pack and headed back to the junction.

"Hey, kid."

Peter froze.

The man had followed him outside. He yanked a thumb over his shoulder. "School's that way."

Peter waved and smiled, trying to act dopey, and changed direction. At the corner, he risked a glance over his shoulder. The man was still watching him.

Peter took off, sudden trickles of sweat chilling the back of his neck. He didn't stop running until he reached the school entrance, then cut through the parking lot.

All he wanted to do was hide for a couple of minutes – maybe crouch between a couple of pick-ups – and figure out an escape route. But beyond the parking lot and the utility buildings, he saw something a whole lot more appealing.

A baseball diamond carved into the lime-green spring grass. And tucked along the third-base line, facing away from the school, an empty dugout.

Peter stood at the top of the rise looking down at the sight. He argued with himself for only a minute. He'd like to be moving, for sure, making time. But what if that guy had called the police? Hitting the road would be risky. Any time he rested he could easily make up at night, since he had a torch now. And he was suddenly tired – bone-dead tired.

Mostly, though, it was the way the field looked so welcoming, as if it were inviting him in. Peter always felt good on a baseball field. And maybe that was a sign – he didn't think he believed in signs, but after the coyotes last night, he wasn't sure he didn't. Peter adjusted his rucksack and loped down the hill.

In the dugout, the familiar mingled scents of leather, sweat, and stale bubble gum wrapped around him like a hug. Peter hurried into his other set of clothes and rubbed a handful of clay-red dirt through his hair – when he left here, he sure wasn't going to look like any description the police might have. He filled his thermos from a water fountain, drank it all down, and filled it again. As he wriggled under the bench, he smiled, realising that Pax would have chosen this same spot – protected, but with a good vantage point – if he wanted a rest.

An hour, that was all, and then he'd cut behind the school and pick up the road again. Enough time that if the police had been called, they would lose interest. He arranged his baseball glove and lowered his head. "Just an hour," he murmured. "I won't even close my eyes."

5

This is my territory.

Pax was so startled that he nearly toppled from the oak trunk he'd been drowsing on: all day he'd been keeping watch and seen nothing larger than a grasshopper, and now here was a bright-furred vixen. He had never seen another fox before, but he knew: younger and smaller and a female, but fox. Instinct told him also that the way she held her ears and tail erect meant she expected his submission.

I hunt here.

Pax felt an urge to run back to his crude nest and press

himself into the remaining stalks, as if retreating to his pen, but he resisted it – what if his boy came back and he wasn't here? He flattened his ears to show he meant no threat, but that he would not leave.

The vixen paced over, and Pax drew in her scent – as familiar as his own, but also exotic. She sniffed and bristled in distrust at the human scent on him.

Pax had been born with that same instinct as well, but distrust is no match for kindness administered consistently and unmeasured, especially in creatures new to the world. Pax had been only sixteen days old when Peter had rescued him – a fatherless, motherless curl of charcoal fur, his eyes barely opened – and it wasn't long before he'd come to trust the quiet, gangly boy who'd brought him home.

The vixen poked her pointed snout in to sniff him more closely and bristled again.

The scent is my boy's. Have you seen him? Pax shared the most important features of his human – the naked round ears; the towering legs, so improbably long that Pax always feared he would topple over when he ran; the black curled hair that grew to different lengths, then became short again.

No humans are here, but they are approaching. Just then, Bristle's head rose as if jerked on an unseen wire. Her ears pricked, trained on a slight rustling in a nearby tuft of broom sedge. Her rear began to twitch, gathering energy. She sprang high and then, paws tight over her black nose, dived into the grass with a flash of white-tipped tail.

Pax sat up, alert. In a second, Bristle's head reappeared, and in her jaws was a wood rat. She leaped clear of the grass, bit through the rat's neck, then dropped it to the ground.

Orphaned before he'd been weaned, Pax had never eaten raw prey. His hunger rose at the blood-scent, and so did his curiosity. He took a cautious step closer. Bristle growled, and Pax retreated to watch from a safe distance.

He grew hungrier as she crunched bites. He thought of the brimming comfort of his kibble bowl, the pleasure of Peter's hand-fed treats and the ultimate reward: peanut butter. He needed to find his boy. His boy would feed him.

Before he could ask about the approaching humans, Bristle picked up what remained of the rat – a single hind leg with its long tail – and stalked off with it dangling from her jaw. Pax watched as she wove her way between the grass tufts, becoming only flashes of flame and white. Leaving. He was swept by the memory of his humans' car roaring away in its stinging spray of gravel.

Just before she slipped into a fringe of ferns at the wood's edge, she paused to glance at him over her shoulder. At that moment, a sharp snap from the fallen oak startled her. It was followed by a red streak of fur that hurtled from the dried foliage, flew over the weeds, and landed on her back.

Pax flattened himself. He could hear the vixen's yips as she scuffled with her attacker, but they sounded more irritated than afraid. He poked his head up. Bristle pounced on a ball of fur and bit it hard. To Pax's surprise, a smaller, skinnier version of herself unfurled at her paws.

Pax was stunned. Never had he suspected that foxes might soar like birds, whose swooping arcs were not like any movement he himself could achieve.

The little fox flipped to his back and gave his belly in submission, but this seemed only to make Bristle angrier, her chattering now punctuated by jabs and nips. Pax bounded over, overcome by curiosity.

The skinny fox startled at the unfamiliar human scent and looked over Bristle's shoulder. His eyes widened when he spied Pax, and he scrambled to his paws. *Friendly,* he announced to Pax; *brother but not littermate of the vixen. Play!*

Bristle bared her teeth and snarled at her brother. *Dangerous. Stay away.*

Pax ignored Bristle's warning posture and met the greeting. *Friendly. You FLEW! BIRD?*

The little fox bounded back to the fallen oak, then sprang on to its trunk. One fork of the dead tree angled up. The small fox walked lightly along its length. He looked down to make sure Pax was watching.

Pax dropped and tucked his paws under his chest, but it was hard to keep from leaping on to the tree to try it himself. He had climbed the walls of his pen, of course, but he'd never been higher than its six feet. His brush twitched.

The vixen stalked a few steps away and then dropped to the ground. She rolled on to her side to gaze directly up at her brother, her love for him obvious now. *He was the runt. He's small, but he's tough. I don't want him with me when I hunt. But he follows me.* She tossed her head and growled at Pax, as though blaming him for her brother's play.

The runty little fox stepped out along the branch, tail poised for balance, then coiled himself and leaped out over the heads of the earthbound foxes. He landed in a clump of burdock beside the road and then burst out covered in burrs. He tore around in mad circles, as if soaring had filled him with an excess of joy that had to be spent through his legs, and then flung himself on to the ground to roll out the rest.

His sister pounced on him. *Too close to the road!* While she pulled the burrs from his coat, she scolded him for the recklessness of his flight. But Pax marvelled at it – a good five full-bounds he'd travelled without touching paws to ground. He would try the feat himself one day.

When Runt managed to get to his feet, he lowered his head and nuzzled his sister. She knocked him back to the ground, only mock-rough this time, and then sat on him, pinning him down. He struggled a little but never really tried to upset her, and he protested only meekly when she began to groom him.

Pax settled himself a respectful distance away. After a while, her brother now properly subdued and her irritation spent, Bristle retrieved the morsel of rat and dropped it in front of him. She lay down and began to lick her paws, then to clean her face with them.

Pax edged closer, so low that his belly brushed the ground. The company of these two young foxes drew him, whether he was welcomed or not.

Bristle stretched out in a patch of slanting sunlight. Her damp cheeks glistened like the pumpkin-coloured wood of the table where Pax's humans ate their food, brilliant against the white of her sleek throat.

Pax looked over at Runt, who was sniffing the spot where Pax had slept. His coat markings were identical, but not as vibrant. His fur was sparse and tufty in places, and his hip bones protruded at sharp angles. He reared back suddenly and pounced in mock attack.

Pax watched as Runt tossed the toy soldier into the air and then pinned it down, over and over. He had done the same thing as a kit. He trotted over and joined the game, and Runt welcomed him as though they had played together since birth.

Bristle got to her feet. *Bring it here.*

Her brother ignored her for a moment but then, as if he had been judging the limits of his sister's patience, he loped over and dropped the toy at her paws.

Bristle issued a throaty rattle at the soldier. *Human. Leave it. Home. Now,* she ordered her brother.

Runt leaned in to Pax and braced his forelegs.

Bristle sprang back to nip at her brother. *He stinks of*

41

the humans. Remember.

Pax was startled by the image she communicated to her brother then: a cold, howling wind; a mated pair of foxes, struggling with something that reminded Pax of his pen – steel, but with jaws and clamps instead of bars. The steel jaws and the snowy ground were smeared with blood.

Bristle tipped her head to assess the sky and sniff the breeze, which carried the threat of thunderstorms from the south. *Home.*

Runt lowered his tail and began to follow his sister. But then he turned back to Pax, inviting him to come as well.

Pax hesitated. He didn't want to leave the spot his humans would return to. But dark clouds were rolling in, and just then, thunder boomed in the distance. He knew his boy would not venture out during a storm. He didn't want to think of getting drenched by the side of the road. Alone.

He tucked the toy soldier into his cheek and set out after the two foxes.

Bristle turned when she sensed his presence. *One night only, Human-Stinker.*

Pax agreed. He would follow his scent back to the road after the storm. His humans would come for him then. And once he found his boy, he would never leave his side.

*P*eter *recognised the sounds before he was fully awake:* the footfalls of a herd of just-released kids, their hoots, the thumping of their eager fists into gloves. He scrambled out from under the bench and grabbed his stuff. Too late: twenty boys and their coach were streaming down the hill. Up at the parking lot, a bunch of adults were overseeing the dismissal, and some of them wore uniforms. His best option was to join the dozen or so kids who were already scattered over the bleachers, heads bent together in clusters of two and three, and blend in when they left.

Peter climbed the bleachers to the top row and dropped his pack. A kid watching a baseball practice – nothing could be more normal, yet his heart skidded.

Below, the coach started lobbing fungoes into the field. The players were mostly the usual guys you expect to see on a ball field, all muscle and shout. Peter found the one he wanted to watch: a small kid with a straw-coloured crew cut and a bleached-out red T-shirt, playing short-stop. While the rest of the players scrambled around like puppies, this kid was a statue, hands poised waist high, eyes glued to the coach's bat. The instant wood smacked cowhide, he sprang. Somehow he managed to reach every ball that came anywhere near his territory, even though he was so short that he looked like someone's tag-along kid brother.

Peter knew he himself wasn't the kind of kid you'd expect to find on a ball field, either, and he was even less at home in the dugout with all the shoulder punching and trash talking. But a baseball field was the only place where he felt he was exactly where he was born to be.

The feeling that brought Peter was something he had never even tried to describe to anyone else – partly because it felt too private, but mostly because he didn't think he had the words to explain it. "Holy" came the closest, and "calm" was in the mix, but neither was exactly right. For a crazy minute, Peter sensed that the short-stop understood about that holy calm, was feeling it too, right now.

The coach had taken the mound and was tossing puffballs. The batters were hitting sharp liners and grounders, and the outfielders were finally paying attention, or at least facing in the right direction. The short-stop was still the one to watch – he looked like he was stitched together with live wires, gaze steady to the play.

Peter recognised that kind of concentration – sometimes his eyes would actually go dry because he forgot to blink, so focussed was he on every move of every player – and knew it paid off. Like the kid in the red T-shirt below him, Peter *owned* his territory on a ball field. He loved that territory right down to the cut-grass, dry-dust smell of it. But what he loved more was the fence behind it. The fence that told him exactly what was his responsibility and what wasn't. A ball fell inside that fence, he'd better field it. A ball soared over it, and it wasn't his to worry about any more. Nice and clear.

Peter often wished that responsibility had such bright tall fences around it off the ball field, too.

When Peter's mother had died, he'd gone for a while to a therapist. At seven years old, he hadn't wanted to talk, or maybe he just hadn't known how to shrink that kind of loss into words.

The therapist – a kind-eyed woman with a long silver braid – said that was okay, that was perfectly okay. And for the whole session, Peter would pull little cars and trucks from a toy box – there must have been a hundred of them in there; Peter figured later that the woman had cleaned out a toy store for him – and crash them together, two by two. When he was finished, she would always say the same thing: "That must have been hard for you. Your mum gets in a car to go buy groceries, a regular day, and she never comes home."

Peter never answered, but he remembered a sense of rightness about those words, and about the whole hour – as if he was finally where he should be, and there was nothing else he should be doing except crashing those little cars and hearing that it must have been hard for him.

Until one day, the therapist said something else. "Peter, do you feel angry?"

"No," he'd said quickly. "Never." A lie. And then he'd gotten off the floor and taken a single green-apple Jolly

Rancher from the brass bowl by the door, exactly the way he did at the end of every session – that was the deal the kind-eyed therapist had made with him: whenever he'd had enough, he could take a sweet and the session would be over – and left. But outside, he'd kicked the sweet into the gutter, and on the way home, he'd told his father he wasn't going back again. His father hadn't argued. In fact, it had seemed a relief to him.

But not to Peter. Had the nice therapist known all along he'd been angry that last day, that he'd done something terrible? That as punishment, his mother hadn't taken him to the store? And did she blame him for what happened?

A few months later, Peter had gotten Pax. He'd come across a fox run over by the side of the road near his house. So soon after watching his mother's coffin lowered into the ground, he'd felt an unshakable need to bury the body. As he'd looked around for a good place, he'd found the den, filled with three cold, stiff kit bodies and one little ball of grey fur still warm and breathing. He'd tucked Pax into his sweatshirt pocket and brought him home, and said – not asked, *said* – "I'm keeping him." His dad had said, "Okay, okay. For a while."

The kit mewed piteously all through the night, and

hearing him, Peter had thought that if he could visit the kind-eyed therapist again, he'd smash those toy cars together all day and all night, all day and all night, forever. Not because he was angry. Just to make everybody see.

Thinking about Pax made the old anxiety snake tighten around Peter's chest. He needed to get moving again, make up some time. The practice was breaking up now, boys loping in from the field, shedding equipment as they streamed past the dugout. As soon as the field was clear, he dropped from the bleachers, pulled his rucksack down, and hitched it over his shoulders. Just as he set out along the diamond, though, he saw the short-stop.

Peter hesitated. He should take off, try to blend in with the stragglers leaving the school grounds. But the rest of the team had left this kid to bag up the equipment and walk back alone, and Peter knew how that felt. He picked up a couple of balls and handed them over. "Hey."

The boy took the balls with a cautious smile. "Hey."

"Nice play. The last liner? That ball had hair."

The boy looked away and scuffed at the dirt, but Peter could see he was pleased. "Yeah, well, the first baseman made it look cleaner than it was."

"Nah, you *planted* that ball. Your first baseman would

49

be lucky to catch a cold by himself. No offence."

The boy gave Peter a real grin. "Yeah. Coach's nephew. You play?"

Peter nodded. "Centre field."

"You new here?"

"Oh . . . I don't live here, I . . ." Peter nodded his head vaguely south.

"Hampton?"

"Yeah, Hampton, right."

The boy's face closed. "Scouting before Saturday's game? Jerk." He spat and walked back to the dugout.

As he left the school grounds, Peter congratulated himself on his quick thinking, covering his runaway tracks. But somehow he felt kind of bad anyway. Somehow he felt lousy, actually.

He shrugged the feeling off – what was it his dad said about feelings, something about a quarter and a cup of coffee? – and checked his watch. Four fifteen. He'd lost over three hours.

Peter pressed faster, but when he came to the town square again, he crossed to the opposite side from the hardware shop and forced himself to walk at an even pace past a library, past a bus station, past a café. Then he counted off a thousand steps before he risked lifting his head.

When he did, he checked his watch again. Four fifty. His grandfather was probably packing up his stuff now. Peter imagined him walking to his rusty blue Chevy, fitting the key into the ignition.

And with that image, his anxiety struck, knocking the breath right out of him. He scaled a low wooden fence and dropped into scrubby brush. He pushed in a good safe thirty feet, until the saplings rose up taller than he was, until his anxiety let him breathe right again, before turning to parallel the road. It was rougher going now, but fifteen minutes later he reached it: the highway.

Peter shadowed the entrance ramp, crouching low, then, at a break in traffic, ran down the culvert, scaled the chain-link fence, and dropped to the other side, his heart beating hard. He'd made it.

He loped into the trees, keeping an eye out for a likely place to cut west. And in just a few minutes, he found one: a dirt road running perpendicular to the highway. Well, not much more than an old wagon path, to be honest, but it was heading in the right direction and would be easy walking even at night. He turned in.

For a short while the trees beside him grew denser as he walked, and only birdcalls and squirrel rustlings broke the silence. Peter realised he might have seen the last of civilisation for a while. The thought lifted him.

But a few minutes later the road turned a corner and began to run along an old pasture dotted with gnarled fruit trees in ragged bloom. A stone wall bordered the field, and a low barn stood at the far corner. There were no lights on in the barn, no car or truck beside it. Still, Peter's heart crashed. The barn looked freshly painted, and some of the roof shingles were the raw pink of new wood. This was the road to someone's home. Worse, it might lead to a bigger road the atlas had been too old to show. In any case, it wasn't a shortcut across the hills.

Peter dropped his pack and sank into a narrow jog in the stone wall, exhausted and starving. He tugged his boots off and peeled down his socks. Two bad blisters throbbed on each heel. They were going to kill when they broke. Peter dug out his extra pair of socks from the bottom of the rucksack and worked them on over the first pair. He rested his head back against the rough stone, still giving off a little warmth from the day's sun, which was now hovering just over the line of trees, bathing the field in a peach-coloured glow.

He pulled the raisins out and ate them one at a time, taking small sips of water in between. Then he opened two packets of string cheese and took four crackers from the sleeve. He ate as slowly as he could, watching the sun over the orchard, surprised to find that he could actually mark its sinking movement. How had he lived twelve years and never known this about sunsets?

Peter laced his boots. Just as he started to rise, he caught sight of a deer, which bounded into the orchard from the woods beyond. He held his breath as the orchard filled – fourteen deer in all. They began to graze, and a few nibbled delicately at the low branches of the trees.

Peter squatted back down, and the closest one, a doe with a spindly spotted fawn beside her, turned her head to look directly at him. Peter raised his palm slowly, hoping to let her know he meant no harm. The doe moved between Peter and her fawn, but after a while she dipped her head into the grass again.

And then the clear twilight air was split by the screech of a saw biting through wood from behind the barn. The herd startled in unison and peeled away into the darkening woods, their white tails flashing. Before she bounded off, the doe sent another look straight at Peter, one that seemed to say, *You humans. You ruin everything* . . .

Peter took off. Back at the highway, half the cars had their headlights on now, and it seemed they were all trained directly on him. He ducked off the road.

The ground there was spongy and smelled of peat. He was just debating about risking the flashlight when his foot sank with a splash. He grabbed an overhanging branch and pulled himself out, but it was too late – he could feel cold swamp water seeping into his boots. Peter cursed. Not bringing more socks – another mistake. It had better be the last of the trip.

And then, clambering back to higher ground, he made another, much worse, mistake.

His right foot caught on a root and he fell. He heard the bone break – a soft, muffled snap – at the same time he felt the sharp stab. He sat panting with the stunning pain for a long moment. Finally he pulled his foot free and unlaced his boot, wincing at each motion. He eased down the wet socks, and what he saw made him gasp: his foot was swelling so fast that he could actually see it.

Peter rolled his socks back up, nearly crying out at the pain it caused, then gritted his teeth to work his foot back into the boot before it could swell any more. He crawled to a tree and pulled himself upright. He tested his weight on his foot and nearly collapsed again. The pain was far worse than anything he'd felt before – it made the broken thumb feel like a mosquito bite in comparison.

He couldn't walk.

*P*ax squirmed in pleasure at the solid, warm weight of another's body nestled against his. Half awake, he sniffed to draw in the comforting scent of his boy. Instead of human, though, he found fox.

He woke fully then. Curled against him, snoring, was the vixen's brother. Runt whimpered and fluffed his tail over his snout, still asleep.

Pax pulled himself up sharply. He had no practice at dominance, but the situation left him no choice. *Go back to your den.* When Runt tried to nestle into his chest, Pax nipped him on the shoulder.

Runt shook himself awake and rolled to his feet. He didn't duck his head in submission, and he made no move to
leave. *Play,* his position invited instead.

In other circumstances, Pax would have welcomed the good-natured little fox's company. But he had no interest in tangling with Bristle again, and in fact he had no interest in anything besides getting back to his humans.

Pax fetched the plastic soldier he'd cached and dropped it as an offering, then warned him away again. After a final pleading look, Runt took the toy in his mouth. Pax followed him out and watched until he slipped into a hole a few tail lengths away.

When the thunderstorm had hit – short but violent, with whole sheets of sky splitting open in wrathful cracks – Pax had worked his way into the shallow entrance of an abandoned den not far from the one Bristle shared with her brother before taking measure of his surroundings. Now, in the pale light of the half-moon, he took a moment to survey them.

The hillside faced south. Here the roots of the trees seemed to claw at the sandy soil like the brown knuckles of clenched fists. Tucked among them, Pax saw three den entrances.

Above this hillside, the forest rose to the north and west, back to the road. Below, a vast grassy valley sloped away. It was an ideal location: the hillside perch provided little cover for approaching predators, while the line of trees protected the foxes from the north winds. The meadow smelled abundantly of life.

As Pax took all this in, a tension deep within him loosened. It was the same way he'd felt as a kit when, after he'd pushed his food dish to the farthest corner of his boy's nest room three times, Peter had finally understood to leave it there. Away from the cold north wall, and with a view of the door where the father entered, sometimes in anger. *Safe.*

But this place was not safe for him. Bristle had warned him that in this same meadow lived an older fox and his mate. He was already facing a challenger from outside and would not tolerate the presence of another lone male. And just then Pax saw a movement below him – a broad-shouldered alpha with black and grey fur emerged from the brush halfway down the slope and marked a sapling beside him. The big fox began to groom, but with a paw still to his ear he suddenly pricked his snout into the breeze. Pax bolted up the hill and plunged into the forest undergrowth.

He picked up his own scent easily although it had rained hard. Stopping only for quick licks of water from the leaves, he followed it back to the road.

There, Pax caught the lingering scent of the military transport caravan from the day before, but no other traffic had passed since then. He settled himself on the fallen oak trunk again to wait.

Morning brought the shimmery buzz of insect clouds and the chatter of waking birds, but still no traffic sounds on the road. As the sun rose hot and dry, it burned off the rain droplets that had hung from every green shoot.

Pax was aware of his hunger now, but his thirst was worse – he'd had nothing to drink since leaving his humans' house. His throat was parched and his tongue swollen and thick. He felt dizzy whenever he shifted his position. A hundred times a thin scent of water drifted past him, but he never considered abandoning his post for its promise. His humans would come back here. He dug his claws into the wood and strained for the sound of a vehicle on the silent road. An hour passed, and then another. Pax dozed and woke and remembered, dozed and woke and remembered. And then the wind brought news of something approaching.

A fox. The same male he'd seen earlier, the one Bristle had warned him about. The fox's gait was deliberate, showing neither hesitation nor wasted energy. The way his greyed coat draped his frame announced that he was old. As he drew close, Pax saw that even his eyes were clouded grey with age.

After offering his scent, Grey settled himself on the grass beside the fallen trunk. He made no move to elevate himself, indicating that he meant no threat. *You carry the scent of humans. I lived with them, once. They are approaching.*

A sudden hope rejuvenated Pax. *Have you seen my boy?* He described Peter.

But Grey had seen no humans at all since the time he had lived with them in his youth. And that was in another place – a dry, stony land of long winters and low sun, distant. *The approaching humans are coming from*

the west. They are bringing war. The crows who have seen
them do not describe any youth.

The news weakened Pax. He swayed and nearly lost
his grip on the trunk.

You need water. Follow me.

Pax hesitated. His humans could come at any time.
But his need for water was urgent. *Is it nearby? Can I hear
the road from this water?*

Yes. The stream passes beneath the road. Follow me.

Grey's manner – confident but not threatening –
calmed Pax. He dropped from his perch and followed.

Soon they came to a deep gash in the earth, from
which rose the scents of water and of things that grew
in rich mud. Pax peered over the edge and saw a silver
brook, studded with black stones, glinting between green
reeds and purple blossoms. Grey began to angle down
cautiously. Lured by the scent of water, Pax scrambled
past him, straight down the cut. Halfway there, he lost his
footing and skidded the rest of the way.

When he righted himself, he stared. The water
tumbled past him as if from a vast faucet, larger by far
than even the spout that poured water into the great white
tub his boy bathed in. He dipped his head. The water was

cold and tasted of copper and pine and moss. It rushed into his mouth as if it were alive. It stung his teeth and drenched his mouth and throat. He drank and drank, and he didn't step away until his belly was taut.

Grey joined him, drank, and then invited Pax to rest with him.

Pax cocked his head to listen intently to the still-silent road above the culvert. *I must be at the road when my humans come for me.*

Grey eased himself to the ground and stretched out. *That road was blocked yesterday by the war-sick.*

Pax thought back to the vehicles that had passed the day before, the ones that smelled like his boy's father's new clothing. It was true that the road had been unused since then. But it didn't matter. *My boy will return for me there.*

No. The crows report this: the road is closed.

Pax paced from stone to stone, thrashing his tail as he worked the puzzle. The answer came: *I will go to my boy at our home.*

Where is your home?

Pax circled to be sure, although there was no question: he felt the pull of his home strongly from only one direction. *South.*

Grey did not seem surprised. *There are vast human colonies there. When the war-sick arrive here, my family will have to move nearer to those colonies or go north, into the mountains. Tell me about the humans there. How they are to live beside.*

Again, the old fox's comportment soothed Pax. He came back and sat. *I have seen many from a distance, but I know only two.*

Are they false-acting, like the ones I knew?

Pax did not understand.

Grey rose to his haunches, agitated, and shared the behaviour he had seen: A human turning away a starving neighbour, acting as if there were no food in his larder when it was full. A human feigning indifference to a mate she'd chosen. A human enticing a sheep from its flock with a soothing voice and then butchering it. *Your humans do not do these things?*

Immediately Pax thought of his boy's father pulling him from the car, his voice mimicking a sense of regret Pax knew was false by the burst of lie-scent he'd given off.

He turned back to the brook. As it spilled over a pair of stones, the current split and then reunited in a liquid silver braid. Pax was struck by a memory.

Not long after his boy had rescued him, when he was still a skittish kit, a stranger had come to the door. Pax had watched from under a table as his boy's father had greeted a woman with a long silver braid streaming over one shoulder. His smile showed all his teeth, which Pax had come to understand meant, *Welcome; I am glad to see you; I wish you no harm.* But beneath the smile, the man's body was rigid with anger and fear.

Pax had been confused by this fear – the small woman was projecting nothing but kindness and concern. She kept repeating the word Pax had already come to associate with his boy – "Peter" – in a pleading tone. The man's full-teeth welcome smile remained frozen in place, but the room had flooded with the bitter scent of deception as he answered her. His chest had been puffed out in threat as he shut the door hard against her.

Pax turned to the older fox. *I have seen it. Not in my boy, never in him. But it's true of his father.*

The old fox seemed to age as he took this in. With visible effort he rose on his haunches. *Are they still careless? They were careless where I lived with them.*

Careless?

They plow a field and they slaughter the mice living there

64

with no warning. They dam a river and leave the fish to die. Are they still careless that way?

Once, when Peter's father was about to cut down a tree, Pax had watched Peter climb it to take down a nest and move it to another tree. On cold days, Peter brought fresh straw to Pax's pen. Before he himself ate, he always made sure Pax had water and food. *My boy is not careless.*

The old fox seemed relieved by this news. But only for a moment. *When war comes, they will be careless.*

What is war?

Grey paused. *There is a disease that strikes foxes sometimes. It causes them to abandon their ways, to attack strangers. War is a human sickness like this.*

Pax jumped to his feet. *The war-sick – they will attack my boy?*

War came to the land where I lived with humans. Everything was ruined. There was fire everywhere. Many deaths, and not only of the war-sick, the adult males. Children, mothers, elders of their own kind. All the animals. The men who were sick with the disease spilled their chaos over everything in their path.

This same thing is coming?

Grey raised his head in a howl that turned the air itself

to sadness. *West of here, where the war is already, where the humans are killing each other, the land is completely ruined. The crows carry the news. The rivers are dammed. The earth is scorched bare; not even briars will grow. Rabbits and snakes, pheasants and mice . . . all creatures killed.*

Pax leaped to the path. He would find his boy. Before this war came.

Grey followed. *Wait. I will travel south with you to search for a new home. Follow me back first.*

Back to the meadow? No. The vixen warned me not to return.

The vixen will never welcome you, because you have lived with humans.

Pax then caught a quick flash of the same scene he'd watched pass between the vixen and her brother: a cold, howling wind; a mated pair of foxes in great distress; a cage of steel clamps; blood staining snow. And then, abruptly, nothing.

But she's not dominant. Follow me back. We will rest and eat, then leave tonight.

8

*T*he sound Peter most loved in the world – the leather-to-leather smack of ball in glove – was so real in his dream that he smiled as he opened his eyes. And then yelped in shock.

A woman stood over him, tossing a baseball into a glove. She wore patched overalls with faded bandannas knotted along the straps, and her hair was a spiked mess that shook as she cocked her head to study him.

He scrambled backward along rough wooden floorboards, crying out again, this time at the pain shooting up from his right foot. It all came back fast. In rising panic, he looked around for his pack. There it was, behind the woman, its contents strewn across the floor.

She came closer and thumped the ball into the glove a little harder.

His ball, and *his* glove, Peter realised. The ball that had been in his pack. The glove he'd been *sleeping* on. He strained up. "Hey! That's my stuff! What are you doing here?"

At that, the woman threw back her head and barked something between a laugh and a snort. She pitched the ball and glove away and crouched down to eye him, one hand wrapped around a clutch of feathers she wore on a rawhide strip around her neck.

This close, Peter could see that she wasn't as old as he'd thought. Not much older than his father, anyway. A single grey streak bolted through her hair, but her skin was smooth. When she narrowed her eyes and snapped her fingers at his face, it dawned on him that the woman might be crazy.

"No. No, no, no. This is *my* barn you broke into, so 'What are you doing here?' would be *my* question."

Peter scooted back. Crazy or not, the woman standing over him had a wall full of hatchets and scythes behind her, and he was one foot short of a running pair. "Okay, right. I hurt my foot last night. I'd passed your barn, and I needed a place to stay, so . . . Look, I'll go."

"Not so fast. What do you mean, you *passed my barn*? This is private property and I'm in the middle of nowhere."

The woman straightened to her full height, and Peter edged back even farther.

"I . . . I was taking a shortcut home from . . ." The practice he'd been to the day before flashed before him. He nodded to his ball and glove. "From batting practice."

"You were coming home through my land from batting practice? Then the first thing I am wondering is why you don't have a bat." She tossed a hand toward his stuff. "Why you carry a roll of duct tape, garbage bags, and a charm bracelet, clothing, food, and water . . . but no bat. Eh, boy?"

The way she said "boy" – silky and stretched out to two syllables – made him realise she had the hint of an accent. Only a hint, as if sometime in her childhood, people around her had spoken a language that was close to singing.

"Well, I . . . I left it. A bat's heavy to carry around."

The woman shook her head again, and this time she looked disgusted. She yanked up the left leg of her overalls. Below the knee, her leg was a rough wooden post. She stabbed it down beside Peter. "Now, this leg. Oh, this leg is heavy, boy. Solid heart pine. But I carry it around, don't I?"

The woman peered down at it and seemed to discover something she didn't much like. She pulled a knife from her belt and, with a flick of her wrist, shaved off a chink from just above where her ankle would have been. Then she straightened to face Peter again, the knife jabbing directly at him. "So let's try one more time, because I am very curious now: If you were at batting practice, how is it you don't you have a bat?"

Peter dragged his gaze up to the woman's face and then back down to the knife. The blade gleamed long and thin, with an evil-looking curve to it. She was probably crazy, all right. Probably worse. His heart stuttered in his chest, and his mouth was a desert, but he managed to answer. "I don't own one."

The woman flashed half a grin and a quick wink. "Better. Yes, that has the feel of truth. What's your name?"

Peter told her.

"So, No-bat Peter, what's this about your foot?"

Peter kept his eyes on the knife as he peeled the sweatshirt from his foot. The pain of just that slight movement shocked him. Shudders racked him, and for the first time he realised how cold he was. "I twisted it."

The woman crouched down, her wooden leg angled out awkwardly. Peter looked away.

"Don't move."

Before he could even register what was happening, the woman slipped the cool blade of her knife inside his sock and with, a quick stroke, slit it open. He pressed his lips together to keep from crying out. His foot was as dark and swollen as an eggplant.

"You walked on this?"

Peter pointed to the branch beside him. "I broke it off. Made a cane." His finger was shaking. He dropped his hand.

The woman nodded again and then cupped her hands around his heel. "I'm going to move this around," she warned. "You ready?"

"No! Don't touch it!"

But the woman began to probe his foot, calling

commands. "Move your big toe. Now all of them. And the foot, side to side." Peter winced at the pain, but he did everything she asked.

"You're lucky," she said, setting Peter's foot down on to his sweatshirt. "A nondisplaced fracture of the fifth metatarsal. That's a single clean break in the outermost bone of the foot."

"Lucky? How is a broken bone lucky?"

The woman reared back, slammed her wooden leg down near his hand, and then stabbed her blade into the wood. "Oh, I don't know . . . let's see . . . how is *only a broken bone* lucky . . ."

"Okay, okay, I get it. Sorry."

She tugged the knife from her leg and pointed it at him. "You're young. You'll be in a cast for maybe six weeks, heal just fine."

"How do you know this stuff? Are you a doctor or something?"

"I was a medic. Another life." The woman hoisted herself up and looked down at Peter as if she'd just put it together. "A runaway." She crossed her arms over her chest and cocked her head at him. "Yes? Are you running away?"

"No! No, I was just out . . . hiking."

She clapped her hands to her ears and frowned. "I'm sorry, I couldn't hear you. My lie detector was going off. Try again: Are you running away from home?"

Peter sighed. "Not exactly."

"Then what, exactly, were you doing last night passing through my land with your extra clothes and your supplies, No-bat Peter?"

"Well, I'm not running away *from* home, I'm running away *to* home."

"Oh, that's a twist. Continue."

Peter looked out the window over the workbench. Tall pines pierced a pale morning sky, and a bunch of crows argued noisily in the top branches. If there were a story he could tell that would get him out of this barn and back on the road to Pax, he would tell it. He would disappear into that day, fractured fifth metatarsal and all. But if such a story existed, he couldn't think what it was. He slumped against the wall. "The war. It's heading for our town. They'll take the river. My dad had to go and serve. My mum died, so it's just us. So he brought me—"

"How old is this father of yours?"

"What? He's thirty-six. Why?"

"Then he didn't *have* to do anything. If there's a draft, it's for eighteen- to twenty-year-olds. Still kids, easy to brainwash. So if your father went, he volunteered. It was his *choice*. Let's start this story off with the truth. That's the rule around here."

"Okay, sure. He *chose* to go. And he brought me to my grandfather's, and—"

"And you didn't like it there."

"That wasn't it. It was . . . uh, could you put that away?"

The woman looked down and seemed surprised to find the knife in her hand. "Such bad manners, Vola," she chided herself. "We've forgotten how to behave with a guest!" She tossed the knife on to the workbench. "Go on."

"Okay. I had a fox. I *have* a fox. We turned him loose. We left him on the side of the road. My dad said we had to, but I should never have done it."

Since the instant they'd driven away, Peter had been tormented by the things he should have said to his father. They all came rushing out now. "I raised him from a kit. He trusted me. He won't know how to survive outside. It doesn't matter that he's 'just a fox' – that's what my father calls him, 'just a fox' as if he's not as good as a dog or something."

74

"Yes, yes. You were plenty angry, so you ran."

"I wasn't angry. I'm not. It's that my fox, he depends on me. I'm going to go back and get him."

"Well, now you're not. Change of plans."

"No. I have to get him and take him home." Peter rolled to his knees, swallowing the gasp of pain that shot from his foot. He grabbed the branch and tried his weight on it for a second, then sank back down, exhausted from just that.

"Now? You still think this? How far away did you leave him?"

"Two hundred miles. Maybe more," Peter admitted.

Vola snorted. "You wouldn't make it two miles now. You'd be nothing but bear bait out there – that is if you didn't die of hypothermia the first night. You won't be able to move enough to keep warm."

She leaned back against the workbench, winding a scarf around a finger, and Peter could tell she was trying to figure something out. She didn't look as crazy now, just deep in thought. And maybe worried. Then she seemed to come to a decision.

"Someone is bound to come looking for you. I can't have that. I need you gone. But I can't send you out like this – I have enough on my conscience. I will bind that foot and give you something for the pain, something that's legal to give a child, and then—"

"I'm not a child. I'm almost thirteen."

Vola shrugged. "And then you will leave. There's a garage not far down the highway. Call this grandfather of yours, have him come get you."

"I'm not going back. I'm going to get my fox."

"Not like this you're not. You cannot bear weight on that broken foot until the bone heals – six weeks at least. Maybe you try again then."

"Six weeks? No, that would be too late. My fox—"

"Remember, boy, I know a little something about travelling on one leg. To get around before that bone heals, you'd have to learn to carry yourself from your shoulders and your arms. You'd have to become strong in new ways. Almost impossible for an adult, never mind a child—"

"I'm not a child!"

Vola swept up a silencing hand. "So you will go back now and have that broken bone set. But first I will bind it for you and fix you something better than that branch to walk with." Vola pushed herself off the workbench and left the barn.

Peter watched her disappear down a pine-framed path, rolling with a limp so deep that it looked painful. Then he crawled across the floor and stuffed his belongings back into his pack. He pulled himself up to the workbench. The effort made him dizzy, and he had to white-knuckle the wood until his head cleared. His foot throbbed fiercely when he was upright, and by testing it slightly he knew he wasn't going to be able to walk on it. Vola would bind it, though. He'd be able to walk on it then. He had to.

He hoisted himself on to the bench to wait.

He hadn't been able to see much of the barn the night before, even with the torch. Now he took it in. The floor was swept bare, with bags of seed and fertiliser stacked neatly by the door. The place smelled of clean hay and wood, and not of animals, although he could hear chickens nearby.

The workbench took up a whole gable wall of the barn. It was lined with small tools and pieces of wood. Opposite, dark against the bright rectangle of the doorway beside it, draped burlap covered a bunch of things mounted on the wall.

Another convulsion of shivers shook him, this time not from cold. The covered mounds were shaped like human

heads. Any number of perfectly harmless things could be hanging on a barn wall, but what they really looked like were human heads.

His throat went dry and his heart began to kick hard. He'd been stupid and careless. Probably the crazy woman was going to let him go — why wouldn't she let him go? — but maybe she wasn't. He found the knife she'd left and wrapped his palm around its smooth grip. Vola had the upper hand in whatever was going to happen between them, but that didn't mean he couldn't defend himself. He slid the blade into his pocket just as she appeared in the doorway.

"Drink this." She handed Peter a mug and set a bowl beside him. Peter sniffed at the mug.

"Cider. There's a measure of willow bark in it, so drink it all."

"Willow bark?"

"Aspirin in the wild."

Peter put the mug down. He wasn't going to drink a crazy woman's brew.

"Suit yourself." Vola took up the bowl, began stirring the green paste inside with her finger.

"What's that?"

"Poultice. With arnica for the bruising and comfrey for the broken bone." She gestured for him to prop his foot on the bench.

The poultice felt cool and soothing as she eased it over the hot, tight skin. She untied a bandanna from her overall strap and wrapped it around his foot, binding it with a second scarf so that it felt secure. Then she straightened up, wiping her hands on her overalls. "How tall are you?"

"Five foot three. Why?"

Vola didn't answer. She rummaged through a stack of lumber, brought several long, narrow pieces over to a pair of sawhorses, and began sawing them into paired lengths. The cut wood smelled fresh and clean. As she nailed short boards across the tops of two longer ones, Peter understood. Crutches. She was making him a pair of crutches. The knife he'd stolen grew heavier across his thigh.

In a few minutes, Vola had angle braced the top boards and screwed on hand rests. She measured the crutches against him, then sawed an inch off the bottom of each.

Then she rolled out an old tire from the corner of the barn. She went to her workbench. She scanned its length. Peter's cheeks burned as she turned to him.

"Did you take my knife?" Her voice had turned dangerous, like something that could burst into flame and peel the roof off the barn.

Peter felt dizzy and his heart began to thud again. He pulled the knife out and handed it to her.

"Why?"

Peter swallowed hard. His words were gone.

"Why?"

"Because . . . Okay, because I was afraid you might kill me."

"Kill you?" She eyed him hard. "What? Because I live out in the woods, that makes me a murderer?"

Peter raised a shoulder toward the wall of bladed tools.

"My tools? I have twenty acres of trees to care for. And I'm a wood-carver. You thought they were weapons?"

Peter looked away, ashamed.

"Look at me, boy."

He turned back.

"Maybe you are not wrong," she said, locking his gaze. "Maybe you see something. Maybe I am" — she raised her hands slowly, pinched her fingers together in front of Peter's face, then suddenly flicked them open — "boom! Dangerous, like that . . . no warning!"

Peter flinched. "No, I'm sorry. I was wrong."

Vola shot a palm at him and spun away. She cut four strips of rubber from the tire, then wrapped them around the crutch tops and grips and secured them with twine in silence. She held the crutches out.

Peter placed one under each arm and eased himself to the floor. It was an immediate comfort to be upright and balanced, with his injured foot safely tucked up.

"Take your weight on your palms. Lift yourself; don't hang. Plant the crutches, then swing through."

Peter began to thank her, but Vola cut him off again. "At the end of my road is the highway. Head left, and in a quarter of a mile you'll come to a petrol station. You figure it out from there." She helped him into his rucksack and then turned away, picked up a block of wood, and began to shave off slices as if he were no longer in the barn.

Peter tried a step toward the door. He wobbled a little, but not much.

"That was a hop," Vola said without looking up. "I said *swing* through. Now, get out of here."

For a moment Peter didn't move. He didn't know where he was headed, only that it sure wasn't back to his grandfather's. Vola turned and leaned toward him, pinched her fingers together, and shot them out at him again. "Go. While you're still safe."

9

*A*pproaching *the meadow from the forest above, Grey* stopped suddenly, nose in the air. *Again.* He lifted his muzzle to test the scent more carefully. *Stronger.*

Pax, already hesitant, tensed.

Grey hurried to the edge of the trees. *A loner is challenging me. He wants this territory, but his display is for the young vixen's benefit – she will choose a mate this winter.*

Pax followed and took in the scene below him. Four foxes dotted the meadow. Bristle and Runt stood together, their black-tipped ears pricked forward warily toward the other two, who faced each other on a ledge of rock, halfway

83

down. One of these was a vixen, darker than Bristle and big-bellied with kits. The other was a large male with rough, tawny fur. His hackles were up and his left ear was split.

Grey barked to announce his presence. The challenger spun off the ledge, an arc of blood spraying from his ear, and bolted down the meadow.

Grey picked his way down the hillside, Pax following. As Grey passed Bristle and Runt, his very presence seemed to calm them, as if he were an unseen hand stroking their backs. As soon as he passed, Runt danced his excitement at seeing Pax, but Bristle curled a lip and hissed.

Pax hurried after Grey. When Grey climbed to the ledge beside his mate, Pax dropped to its base and sat, respectful. Grey's mate greeted him with affection. Then she shared news. *The wind this morning was from the west. It brought the scent of fire. We must move soon.* She looked out at Pax. *The outsider smells of humans.*

Bristle and Runt edged closer, ears cocked toward Grey's response. *He is returning to the humans he lived with in the south. I will travel with him to search for a suitable place to move. He and I will rest, then leave tonight.*

Behind him, Bristle growled again and Pax felt the

urge to run. His boy – he wanted only to find his boy. But instinct told him that he needed rest and food first. He signalled his agreement, and then Grey and his mate glided silently into the green meadow.

Runt bounded over and tumbled into Pax. He dropped the toy soldier from his cheek, inviting Pax to play. Bristle jumped between them and swatted the toy away. *Humans. Remember the danger.*

Runt retrieved the toy and displayed it between his teeth, defiant.

Pax sensed that Runt was now in more trouble than before, and that he was the cause. He'd felt that way often with his boy and the father, and one of his strategies had been to disappear if that would protect his boy from the man's anger. He backed away, but Bristle was not satisfied.

Stay away from the human-stinker, she warned her brother. *Remember the danger.*

Pax took a step closer. *My humans are not dangerous.*

Runt seemed alarmed by this, as if Pax had issued a challenge. He darted uphill toward his den entrance, but his sister was quicker. She blocked him, and when he tried to slink away in another direction, she restrained him with a heavy paw until he stilled in defeat.

All humans are dangerous . . .

Pax's fur ruffled in a shiver at the scene Bristle conjured then: wind, cold and howling and heavy with the threat of snow. Pax recognised that wind – the story she was about to relate would end with blood on the snow and cold steel jaws.

Bristle bared her fangs at Pax and then began.

10

At the jog in the wall where he'd seen the deer, Peter stopped.

There was blood already – he'd stumbled and ripped open the tender web of skin at the base of his thumb on a jagged splinter – and buckets of sweat. His arms trembled from the strain of lifting his weight for only these few minutes, his palms already raw on the rubber grips, and the throbbing in his right foot menaced like thunder, but none of that was what was wrong. It wasn't even the prospect of returning to his grandfather's grim house.

He was going in the wrong direction.

He wheeled round. He stabbed the ground and swung over it, stabbed and swung, until he planted himself in the doorway of Vola's barn again. He drew himself up tall. "No."

Vola's head snapped up. She shot him a warning scowl, but on her face Peter read a flash of something else: fear.

"I'm not going back," he said, more firmly. "Whether you help me or not, I'm going to get my fox."

"Help you?"

Peter moved to the bench and hoisted himself up. "Teach me. What you said about moving from my arms, about getting strong. You learned how to get around on one leg – teach me. You were a medic. Set my bone. Please. I'll do whatever you tell me to." He picked up the cider and drank it down to show his trust. "Then I'll leave. But even if you won't help me, I'm going to get him."

Vola put her hands on her hips and lowered her head to eye him. "A tamed fox, set loose in the wild? You know he might be dead, don't you?"

"I know. And it would be my fault. If he's dead, I need to bring him home and bury him. Either way, I'm going to go back to find my fox and bring him home."

Vola studied Peter as if she were seeing him for the

first time. "So which is it? You going back for your home or for your pet?"

"They're the same thing," Peter said, the answer sudden and sure, although a surprise to him.

"And you're going to do this no matter who tries to stop you? Because it's the right thing for you, at your core?" Vola made a fist and thumped her chest. "Your *core*. Is that true?"

Peter waited before answering, because this woman – maybe crazy, maybe not – had asked it as if the fate of the world depended on it. But the answer was the same as it would have been if he'd blurted it out. The answer would have been the same if he'd waited a lifetime to think it over. He thumped his own chest and felt the muscle of his heart leap. "Yes. In fact, there's nothing else I know at my core."

The woman nodded. "Well, you're twelve. That's old enough to know your own self, I expect. I'm not about to go messing with that. So all right."

"You'll help me?"

"I'll help you." Vola extended her hand to shake. "On three conditions . . ."

11

My brother was born in my mother's second litter. They came early in the season. Last year, spring came late. Snow fell and did not melt; the earth stayed frozen beneath it. I lived nearby; I helped hunt. All day long our parents and I searched for food, because the kits were always hungry. But there was never enough.

Two of his littermates died on the same day. The farm, our mother urged. At the humans' farm, there were always fat mice in the warm barn. At the humans' farm, there were eggs in the chicken coop.

Our father would not risk it.

When her third kit grew too weak to stand, our mother defied him.

Runt raised his head and gave Bristle a pleading look.

Bristle ignored it. *She led the strongest of her new kits — my sister — and me to the humans' farm.*

Runt edged closer and pressed his nose into Pax's shoulder. Instantly the vixen lashed at his cheek, although Pax noted she did not use her claws. Runt dropped to the ground.

The ground around the barn was cleared of snow by many footprints, animal as well as human. The air was rich with the smell of rodents. Our mother headed for a gap in the wooden boards near the base, with us a few tail-lengths behind. Just before she reached it, steel jaws sprang out of the earth with such speed that the air snapped. Our mother screamed. The clamp held her front leg. The more she thrashed, the deeper the metal cut. She began biting at her leg to free it. Every time we tried to come near, she ordered us away.

Our father appeared. He had followed our tracks. He chased my sister and me back into the brush and ordered us to stay there. Then he set to helping our mother.

The scene she conveyed was of two foxes, bonded by both an old love and a new fear, the fear so terrible that their eyes rolled back in their sockets, so vivid that Pax could smell its sharp scent.

Runt began to whimper, a piteous sound that made Pax want to comfort him, but Bristle warned him to keep away.

A human came then, with a stick. Both our parents screamed at us to run home. We stayed. We saw. The human raised the stick, and in front of our eyes our mother and our father burst into blood and fur and shattered bones spattered over the snow.

Runt whined and backed away toward the den again, and again Bristle stopped him.

My sister and I could not leave our parents' bodies. Darkness fell and the next day came, and still we hid in a pile of wood beside the barn. Finally we set out, but that night it began to snow. The snow blotted out all sound and scent. Lost, we crawled under a sweep of pine boughs, and I curled myself around my sister, who was so much smaller. In the morning, she died. When the snow stopped, I saw that we had sheltered beneath the great pine at the top of our ridge. We had been within sight of home.

The image she shared then – her sister's frozen corpse at the base of the mighty pine – seemed to exhaust her.

Why do we have no family, Brother?

Runt turned to Pax. *Because of the humans, we have no family.*

Bristle turned her golden eyes on Pax, inviting a challenge.

If he could have, he would have made her know every kindness of every day with his boy. But the hatred she had for humans was deep and fair. Instead, he offered his cheek in sympathy. Bristle turned away and ordered her brother into the den.

12

"*Y*ou coming in, or am I just holding the door open for the flies?"

Peter dropped his rucksack. He rebalanced himself on the crutches and stared at the log cabin. "These trees grew here."

It hadn't been a question, but Vola nodded and pointed uphill. "Spruce. From the top of Mason's Ridge. Lincoln Logs – is that what you're thinking?"

"Sort of." But it wasn't. Peter reached out to touch one of the logs. What would it feel like to make something so . . . so consequential? To cut timbers and watch them fall out of a clear blue sky and roll them down to a clearing, your hands sticky with sharp-scented pitch, and then to lift them into place, notched and stacked one over another – yes, just like the toys that had been his favourite in kindergarten, the old set in the tall cardboard canister – and end up with *a home*. "You built this?"

"No. Before my time. Now, come in. I don't have all day."

Peter still didn't move. "What are the conditions? You said you'd tell me when we got here."

Vola sighed and stepped back down on to the slab of granite that formed the front step, letting the screen door clap shut. She picked up a jar of seeds, and a cloud of birds fluttered down from the trees to surround her. She filled a feeder that hung from a corner rafter before turning to answer him. "Number one: I don't want anyone coming around here. I live by myself for a reason. You write to your grandfather and tell him whatever it takes to make sure nobody comes around here. Besides, it's only fair you let your family know you're not dead in a ditch somewhere."

Peter reared back so fast that he almost toppled over. The pain that movement caused was searing, but he bit his lip. "No. He'd come and get me. No."

"Condition number one. Non-negotiable."

She scooped a few seeds from the jar and held out her palm. A chickadee left the feeder and settled on her fingertips. He pecked at the seeds, and when they were gone, she tossed him back into the air. She turned back to Peter. "Number two: you're going to tell me why you're carrying that bracelet."

Peter glanced down at his pack and felt his heart clench to protect what was so private. "Why?"

"Because I'm curious about you. And you can tell a lot about a soldier by what he carries into battle."

"But I'm not a soldier. I'm just going home."

"Is that so? Because it sounds to me like you're headed off to fight for something in a place where there's a war. But have it your way – you're not a soldier. Condition two is still this: when I ask, you're going to tell me why you've brought that bracelet with you. Why that particular thing. The truth – that's the rule here. Agreed?"

Peter nodded. His right foot throbbed, his left leg ached from the extra burden, and his shirt was sweat soaked from the exertion of hobbling the hundred yards from the barn, but he stood his ground. "And number three?"

"You're going to help me with something. I see that look. Don't worry – it's just a project needs a second person, that's all. But I'm not ready to tell you what it is yet." She picked up his rucksack. "Inside. It's time to get you off that foot. And I suspect you're hungry, Mr. Not-exactly-running-away-from-home, No-bat Peter."

Suddenly Peter was starving. Still, he hesitated. He pivoted to look at the hills, which the sun was lightening to smoky blue. Pax was out there. He was still so far away.

Vola came up behind him. Peter sensed her raising a hand toward his shoulder and then letting it fall back.

"I know what you're thinking," she said. "But you are not fit to go yet."

Inside, the cabin was bright and smelled faintly of smoke. Vola tapped a pine table, and Peter sat. She draped a blanket over his shoulders, then left and came back with a plastic bag full of ice cubes. She propped his foot on a chair and wedged the ice bag against it. With a washcloth, she cleaned the blood from his hand. Finally, she passed him a cutting board with a loaf of bread and a knife on it.

Peter put it down. "How long will it take?"

"Depends on you." The woman pointed to the bread.

"What, you can't use your hands either? Slice that up."

"How long?"

"You can go when you can hike over rough terrain on those crutches for eight hours a day. Two weeks, I'd guess. Six slices."

"You don't understand. He won't survive!"

Vola lowered her head to glare at Peter. She yanked her thumb to the wall behind him. "Number eleven."

Peter twisted round. A jumble of index cards was pinned to the wall. *"The Gulf Stream will flow through a straw, provided the straw is aligned to the Gulf Stream and not at crosscurrents,"* he read aloud from the one with an *11* scrawled over it. "What's that supposed to mean?"

"It means align yourself, boy."

"Align myself?"

"Figure out how things are, and accept it. You've got a broken foot. Broken. The deal is you stay until I say you're ready. I told you, my conscience is stretched to its limit. So that's your choice: stay here until I say, or go back to your grandfather's now. You change your mind about that?"

"No, but—"

"Then accept it, *eh*? Now slice the *dyableman* bread."

Peter started to argue but then closed his mouth. He wasn't staying for any two weeks, but obedient and helpful was the safest play for now.

He ducked his head and set to work cutting six thick, even slices of bread while Vola slapped a chunk of butter into an iron skillet and snapped on a flame beneath it. Without turning round, she motioned to a shelf above the counter. "Pick yourself something."

Canning jars, stacked three deep, gleamed like a rainbow of liquid jewels along the length of the shelf. Peter read the plain block letters on the labels: CHERRIES, PLUMS, TOMATOES, BLUEBERRIES, APPLES. PUMPKIN, PEARS, GREEN BEANS, BEETS, PEACHES. Braids of dried garlic and chili peppers hung beside the shelf.

"You grow all this?"

Vola nodded, her back still to him.

"The trees that run along your stone wall are in bloom. What are they?"

"Nearest the wall? Peaches."

He pointed to a jar near the end. "Peaches," he said. "Please. Ma'am."

Vola opened a jar and handed him a fork.

"Uh . . . there's a twig in it or something."

Vola reached into the jar, popped the stick into her mouth, sucked the syrup off, pitched the stick over her shoulder into the sink, and rolled her eyes. "Lord. Cinnamon. Eat." She gathered the bread he'd cut with a curt nod of approval. "Cheddar or Swiss?"

"Cheddar, I guess."

Vola straightened. "You guess, boy? You don't *know*?"

Peter shrugged and speared a peach chunk. It tasted as bright and golden as it looked.

Vola seemed to be working up a whole lot more to say about the cheese issue, but then she pressed her lips together, spun round on the point of her wooden leg, and clumped out the back door. She came back in with a slab of cheese a moment later, then set to work wordlessly making sandwiches. Peter heard them sizzle as she pressed them into the hot skillet.

He surveyed the cabin. It wasn't big, but it didn't feel cramped, either. Sunlight flooded in through clean windows, washing the log walls in a honey glow. Two blue-striped armchairs flanked a stone fireplace, and a trunk stacked with books served as a table between them. Small barrels held lanterns, and more hung from the beams.

There were photos on the mantel, a few paintings on the walls, and a basket of yarn beside the armchair. Through an open door by the fireplace, Peter saw the corner of a bed, neatly made with a yellow-checked quilt. It was a surprisingly normal home for a crazy person, yet something was missing. Peter noticed then how quiet it was – silent, actually, except for birdcalls outside and the butter sputtering in the skillet – but that wasn't it. Not exactly. "Hey," he said as it dawned on him. "You don't have electricity."

The woman flipped the sandwiches. "As far as I know, that's not a crime in this country. Not yet, anyway."

Peter tried to think about what he would miss without electricity, but there were too many things to count. He chased out the last bit of peach, the fork rattling against the empty jar. Vola's back was still turned to him, so he lifted the jar to drain the last drops of syrup. "But wait. How'd you get the ice?"

"I've got a refrigerator out on the porch. It's gas. So's the stove and the water heater. I've got everything I need." She set two blue plates down on the table. Peter's mouth watered at the smell of the food, but he waited. Vola wasn't finished, he sensed.

"I have more than everything I need." Vola sat. "I have peace here."

"Because it's so quiet?"

"No. Because I am exactly where I should be, doing exactly what I should be doing. That is peace. Eat."

Peter bit into his sandwich. The cheese was hot and runny all the way through, the bread fried crisp and brown.

He broke off a corner out of force of habit and was about to reach down with it when he remembered — there was no fox under the table. He wondered if Pax was missing him as much as he missed his fox right now. "Don't you get lonely out here?"

"I see people. Bea Booker, librarian. Robert Johnson, bus driver. I have . . . I see people." She got up, brought the frying pan over, and slid another sandwich on to his plate. "Eat."

Peter ate, thinking about what she'd said about peace. When he finished, he licked the buttery crumbs from his fingers. "What do you mean, you're doing exactly what you should be doing? Do you work?"

"Of course I work! The garden is half an acre and the orchard is twice that size. I'm planting beans and okra today. Maybe get to replacing the seal on the well pump. There's always plenty to do here."

"But you don't go to a job, make any money? How do you buy things? Like all those tools in the barn? Like" – he waved around the cabin – "all your stuff?"

Vola hoisted herself on to the counter and then held out her wooden leg and rapped it with the spatula. "My country pays me a little blood money every month in exchange for my leg."

She dropped the spatula into the sink and shook her head. "A *dyableman* deal – turns out my leg wasn't all that valuable to them. Wish they'd told me that before they sent me scouting in a minefield. Because I liked my leg. It was a good leg – not much to look at, maybe, but it worked fine. It ran me clear into the next town when Deirdre Callanan and I set fire to her father's woodshed in sixth grade, and it kicked the smile off Henry Valentine's face when he tried to grab my butt the next year. I could go on. A leg is a very big price to pay. Every day, every single day, I wish I had it back."

"How come you don't get one that's more . . . ?"

The woman stuck her leg out again and tugged up her cuff to assess the wooden post. "Oh, they gave me a prosthetic – a complicated piece of work. Scared the devil out of me whenever I looked down. So I made my own. It's heavy and it's clumsy, but I did some terrible things in the war. I figure I deserve to drag something around."

"You threw it away? A prosthetic leg, you just threw it away?" Peter couldn't help imagining the shocked look on some binman's face.

"Of course not. I wear it. Sometimes. Right now, it's in the garden, on the scarecrow. Scares the devil out of the crows, too, apparently."

She dropped off the counter and jammed a battered straw hat on to her head as if she'd suddenly remembered this garden of hers. "I'll be back before dark. The outhouse is just beyond the two cedars, and there's a tub in the kitchen. Clean up. The porch is yours. Actually, you'll have to share it with François. Keep that leg elevated."

"Who's François?"

Again Vola's short bark of a laugh startled Peter. She tipped her head toward the back door, which led out to a screened porch. "He's probably out there napping right now, lazy old thief." She crossed to the door, looked out, and then nodded. "Come see."

Peter levered himself off the chair and on to the

crutches. Vola held the door open and waved toward a wood bin. Peter saw a pair of dark-ringed eyes peering out at him. He cocked his head to get a better view, and the raccoon cocked his head back.

"François Villon, named after one of the most famous thieves in history. The original was a poet as well as a thief, and such a charmer that every time they arrested him, some admirer pardoned him."

Peter grinned. He crouched to get a better look. "Hey, chuck-chuck-chuck," he called softly, the way he always greeted Pax in the morning. The raccoon eyed him lazily for another moment, then seemed to decide he wasn't interesting and flopped over and closed his eyes.

"Is he wild or tame?"

Vola waved the words off as if they were gnats. "I leave the porch door open. He visits when he wants to, and he's fine company. I feed him, but I don't have to – he stays fat enough on his own. We've come to a little agreement about the chicken coop – he leaves the girls alone, and I scramble him up an egg now and then. He's a companion. That's the best word."

She pointed to a beam spanning the ceiling. "To-morrow you can do some pull-ups. But today, stay off

the leg and keep it elevated – above your heart is best."
She nodded to the refrigerator. "Keep icing it on and
off. I want the swelling down some so I can set that bone
tonight. Mix a spoonful of willow bark in water every few
hours for pain."

Peter nodded, then dropped into a hammock hanging
from the beams, exhausted.

Vola started to leave, but paused in the doorway and
turned round to study him. She crossed her arms over her
chest, an unreadable expression on her face.

"What?"

"Just wondering," she said. "You staying out here on
the porch. What do you suppose that makes you? Wild or
tame?"

13

When Pax awoke, it was late afternoon. The ache that had cramped his belly the past few days was worse, and when he tried to rise, he lost his balance for a second, his muscles trembling.

He surveyed them for injury with a distanced curiosity. Once, when he'd been ill, his boy had forced a pill down his throat. Afterward, his senses had been dulled and his reactions slowed. He felt this same way now.

He dropped to the cool dirt and watched as, below, Grey and his mate emerged from their rests to scent the air, relieve themselves, then set off for food. Bristle sprang out from a den beside him, stopped only to order her brother to stay behind, then trotted off to hunt also.

On the day he'd gotten into the car with his boy, Pax had sensed the tension and refused his morning kibble, so it had now been three full days since he'd eaten. Although Pax had never seen death, he understood that it awaited him if he did not find food. This thought produced no sense of urgency and drifted away. A second thought, however – that he must find his boy and see him safe – stirred him to rise again, first bracing himself on his forelegs before straightening his haunches.

After a moment his head cleared. He wandered past the dens Bristle and Runt shared. There he smelled caches of game buried in the soft earth, but they were marked with powerful warning scents, so he did not dig them up. Farther out, a few gnawed-over carcasses were discarded to be scoured clean by lower-ranking scavengers. Pax began to poke through the carrion. Only the tail end of a marsh rat held any meat at all. Too rancid and gristly even for the crows, it was crawling with maggots.

Pax lowered his head to the remains. He opened his jaw, but the smell sent him reeling back. This was not food.

He staggered back a few steps and buried his muzzle in

a patch of new clover, chewing the sprouts to cleanse the foul odour from his sensitive nasal passages. He swallowed and then began to feed tentatively. The act of eating was a comfort to his shrunken belly, although a false one – the clover wouldn't strengthen him. After a few mouthfuls, the clear thought arose again: he must find his boy.

Just then, he heard something tear through the grass. Before his sluggish senses could respond, he felt a solid weight plow into him.

Runt pounced on top of Pax, crowing at his successful ambush. When Pax didn't move to shake him off, Runt began to examine him. Pax lay still while the smaller fox sniffed and licked him, too weak to waste energy batting him away.

Unwell?

Pax closed his eyes against the low-glancing sunlight and did not respond.

Runt bounded off and came back a few minutes later with a worm hanging from his jaw. He dropped it at Pax's paws.

Pax shrank away, but the thoughts he'd had earlier surfaced again. He had to find his boy. He could avoid death if he ate. Pax picked up the worm and bit into it.

Unused to the taste of live flesh, Pax retched and twisted away.

Runt dug up another worm and dropped it in front of Pax, and this time Pax got to his feet and took a few steps before sinking back down.

Runt followed and nudged him. *Eat.*

Pax mustered as much dominance as he could. *Leave.*

The younger fox gazed at the older one for a moment, then turned and trotted into the grass. Relieved, Pax laid his head on his paws. He did not have the energy for resistance now. But Runt reappeared after a few moments, something round in his mouth. He dropped his gift and it broke open.

Egg. The scent called up a sharp memory. Once, when he was very young, Pax had found a hard white orb while exploring his humans' kitchen counter. He'd batted at it, thinking it was one of his boy's playthings. It had rolled on to the floor and cracked open, spilling its delicious secret.

Peter's father had come in while he was still licking at the last drops and smacked him away. His flank had stung from the blow, but that egg had been worth it. Since then, Pax managed an exploratory visit to the kitchen counter every time he was left alone, looking for more of them. A few times he'd gotten lucky.

The quail egg Runt had brought was smaller, its speckled shell flecked with dried grass, and it smelled gamier than the ones his humans ate. But there was no mistaking it. Egg.

Pax rose. Runt backed away to allow Pax to lap up the yolked prize. He licked the grass clean of every drop, then looked up, eager to express his gratitude.

Runt was gone, but in a few moments he came back, two more eggs held carefully in his mouth. Pax devoured them. Runt left and returned twice more. Pax ate steadily, until finally, seven eggs swelling his shrunken belly taut, he dropped to the sandy apron in front of the dens and closed his eyes.

Runt leaped on to a gnarled root above the dens. He drew himself up to his full height. And while Pax slept, the ragged little runt kept watch.

14

*P*eter recognized Vola's footsteps — *the hard wooden stamp followed by the softer shoed footfall* — and dropped the logs back into the wood bin. He braced himself in the cabin doorway, watching Vola pump water into the kitchen sink.

"You stayed off that foot?"

"Pretty much." Actually, he'd gotten up at least a dozen times to do pull-ups on a beam and he'd lifted logs for half an hour. His arms were sore and his foot hurt a lot when it wasn't raised, but he hadn't been able to lie around doing nothing knowing Pax was still out there.

Vola began lathering up her hands without turning round. "You write that note?"

Peter pulled the crutches to his sides. Already he felt more secure when they were tucked under his arms. "I did, but—"

"No buts. You write once a week. The bus driver friend I told you about, Robert Johnson – I ask him, he'll mail them from different spots along his route. First condition, remember?"

Peter tried a sharp turn, wobbled, but righted himself. He swung through another turn – smoother.

"All right?"

"Okay."

"Good." Vola hung the dish towel on its peg, crossed to the fireplace, and began shredding newspaper on to the grate. "Let's move to the second condition, then. That charm bracelet you carry. I'm guessing it was your mother's. Why do you carry it with you? Why that particular thing?"

Peter felt his body go instantly rigid the way it always did whenever anyone asked about his mother, as if it had to freeze to decide whether it was okay to talk about her or not. Usually with strangers it wasn't, so he was surprised when his hands relaxed their grip on the crutches a little and his throat eased open.

"She always wore it. She'd hold her wrist up so I could play with it when I was a baby. I don't remember that, but I've seen a picture. I do remember her telling me about it, though. About the charm, I mean. It's a phoenix. That's a special bird. It's red and gold and purple, coloured like sunrise, and it—"

"Rises from the ashes. I know what a phoenix is."

"Right. But out of its *own* ashes. That's the part my mum cared about."

"Its own ashes?"

"When it gets worn out, it builds itself a nest high in a tree, away from everything." Peter stopped. It suddenly occurred to him that Vola's cabin felt like a nest. He circled on the crutches to look around. Yes. A secret, protected nest, surrounded by trees. Away from everything.

He turned back to Vola, who was cross-stacking kindling. He hoped she hadn't read his mind. "So the phoenix fills the nest with its favourite stuff – myrrh and cinnamon is what's in the story, I think. Then the nest ignites, burning the bird's old body. And the new bird rises up out of the old bird's ashes. My mother loved that.

She said it meant that no matter how bad things got, we could always make ourselves new again."

Vola didn't respond. She touched a match to the shredded paper and watched as it caught fire. Her face looked grim in the light of the new flames. She added two logs and then a third. "Go try those crutches outside while there's still some light," she said without looking up.

Peter opened the front door and navigated the step, relieved to get away. He didn't have a clue what he'd said wrong. Living in the woods all alone probably made a person weird. But she was right that he needed to practice outside. He'd lost a whole day now, a whole day. Maybe he did need some time to train and heal, but he was leaving as soon as he could.

He left the cleared yard and headed to where the uneven ground was snarled with roots and brush. It took a torturously long time to circle the cabin. His second turn around was a little faster, and by the fifth circuit he felt almost comfortable, but he was bathed in sweat when he swung back inside.

The cabin was quiet except for the gentle crackling of the fire. Vola sat in an armchair, sewing something yellow. The quiet and the way the setting sun seemed to wash the cabin in peace, as if everything were right with the world, suddenly felt mocking to Peter.

Everything was *wrong* with the world – another day had passed when Pax had been out there alone. Another night was coming when he would be cold. Probably hungry and scared, too. And what if he hadn't found water?

He took a lurching swing across the room. Halfway across, one crutch caught on a rug, and he had to stab the other into the wall to keep from crashing into a lantern.

"Shorter steps. You'll get the hang of them after a while."

"After a while? My fox will be dead in a while." He dropped the crutches and sank to the chair at the kitchen table. "What's the point, anyway? How is this supposed to work out?"

Vola dropped her sewing. "What do I look like – a Magic 8 Ball?" She went out to the porch and came back with a bag of ice; then she lifted Peter's foot to a chair and arranged the ice over it. "I don't have your answers."

The sight of his useless foot reminded him of everything he couldn't do now. He looked away. "Why not? Aren't you supposed to be wise and all? Living out here by yourself, with your . . . with all these" – he threw his thumb toward the jumble of notes tacked on the board behind him – "all these philosophy bingo cards? You're supposed to be wise, at least, aren't you? Or witchy or something."

Peter almost didn't recognise himself, back-talking the woman like this. He felt as if he were short-circuiting – as if his impulses were leaping directly out of him without passing through his brain. But once again he wasn't where he should be, and now his foot was too wrecked to get him there, and Pax was still out there alone.

Vola pulled a bucket out from a cupboard and set it in the sink. "Philosophy bingo cards." She looked only mildly insulted. "I'm trying to figure out my own life. I don't have your answers."

"So who does? And don't say my father, because he's a little absent these days." *And because he caused all this.* Peter hardened his jaw against saying the words and forced himself to breathe slowly. He wasn't angry. He was just frustrated. Anyone would be. Sudden tears threatened – what was wrong with him lately? – and he knuckled his eyes.

Vola started over toward him, then seemed to change her mind. She backed away to lean against the kitchen counter. "You are angry," she said simply, as if she were noting he had dark hair, or the sun was going down.

"I'm not angry." But he forced his fists open and counted ten slow breaths, fighting it the way he always did. Because what if he was like his father, with that threatening kind of anger, the kind that was always simmering, the kind that could boil over at any time and hurt everyone in the way? The apologies afterward never healed the damage.

He squeezed his eyes shut against the tears still crowning. "I'm not angry. It's just that I didn't choose it. I didn't choose for there to be a war. I didn't choose for my father to join up. I didn't choose to leave my home. I didn't choose to go to my grandfather's. And I sure didn't choose to abandon an animal I took care of for five years."

"You're a kid. You don't get a lot of choices. I'd be angry, too. *Dyableman* angry."

"I told you, I'm not angry!" Peter gulped in a sob that somehow escaped as a twisted laugh. He was short-circuiting again. "And you're in love with that word, you know."

"What are you talking about, boy?"

"*Dyableman*. What is it – a swear? You're in love with the word *dyableman*." His wiring felt totally fried. "If we were in second grade, I'd tell you you're so in love with that word, you should marry it!"

She squawked, a loud crow's caw. "But you're right!" she said. "I should get down on one *dyableman* ruined knee and ask that word to marry me!"

"You should!" Peter agreed, kind of hysterical now. "You should put a *dyableman* ring on its *dyableman* finger!" He wiped his face off and watched Vola as she came over and took the seat across from him.

"My grandfather swore in his first language. It drove my grandmother crazy, because she didn't speak it. But she sang in Italian when she cooked, so ..." Vola lifted a finger to stroke the feathers bunched at her throat. "I carry many traits," she said quietly.

And then she went silent for a while, holding his gaze the whole time. In their silence, Peter felt they were saying something important. Something about the long, dark tunnel he felt narrowing around him.

"I was counting on finding Pax in a week, maybe ten days." He looked down at his foot. "Now ..."

"Pax? That's his name? It means 'peace,' you know."

Peter knew that – lots of people had told him. "But that's not why I named him. First day I brought him

121

home, I left him for a minute, just a minute, so I could get him some food. When I got back, I couldn't find him – he'd crawled into my rucksack and fallen asleep. It had the word 'Paxton' sewn on the label. I was seven then, and I figured, *'Paxton,' that's a good name.* It had an X in it, like 'fox,' you know? But now . . ."

"But now what?"

"Now he's all alone because of a war. I let him go because of a war. War, not peace. What's that called? Irony? Whatever, now it's a terrible name. He'll probably die because of a war."

"Maybe yes, maybe no. He could survive. It's spring. Plenty of food, I'd think."

Peter shook his head. "Foxes teach their kits to hunt when they're about eight weeks old. I found him way before that – he was maybe two weeks old, the vet figured. He could run across a dozen mice sitting up on little plates, and he probably couldn't catch them. All he's ever had is kibble and the scraps I'd let him swipe."

"Well, what kind of scraps? Anything he'd find out there?"

Peter shrugged. "He's crazy for peanut butter. He likes hot dogs. Loves eggs. No, unless he stumbles into someone's picnic, he'll starve. He'll find water, I figure, and he can probably go a week without food, but after that . . ."

Peter dropped his head to his hands. "I let it happen. I didn't choose any of it, but I didn't fight it, either. I don't know why I didn't fight it."

Except, of course, he did know. When his father had first dropped the order about Pax, Peter had steeled himself and said, "No. I won't do it." But his father's eyes had flared with that flash-fire anger, and his fist had jerked up, stopping only at the last split second to knuckle Peter's cheek in a gesture that carried enough threat to set Pax on growling alert.

Peter's own fists had come up, and the rage he'd felt at his father had scared him more than the threat itself.

He heard his grandfather's words now – *our apples don't fall far from the tree* – and he felt sick and afraid all over again. He dropped his gaze to the worn pine table to hide the shameful headline he felt burning across his face.

Vola reached over and cupped the top of his head with both hands. Peter froze. Except for an occasional "attaboy" shoulder shake from his father or a casual arm punch from one of his friends, no one had touched him since his mother. Vola paused, as though she knew he needed time. Then she pressed down firmly.

It was a strange thing to do, but Peter didn't pull away, didn't move a muscle, didn't even draw a breath. Because at that moment her strong grip was the only thing keeping him from flying apart.

"Well, that's over now," she said. "Isn't it."

She rose. "I may not have your answers, boy, but I do know one true thing about you. You need food – a lot of food. You're twelve, you've slept out in the cold, and you've got a bone to heal. I'm going to set that bone now. Then I'm going to start cooking and you're going to start eating, and neither one of us is going to stop until you say so. Got it?"

Peter's belly was suddenly a hollow, snarling crater. "Yes, ma'am, I've got it."

Vola rummaged under the sink and drew out a sack of plaster. Peter watched her sift some into the bucket and then pump in some water. Then she brought over the thing she'd been sewing. "Foot up."

Vola propped a pillow under his knee and worked a quilted sleeve over his leg, like an open-toed sock.

He recognized the yellow-checked material. He glanced into the bedroom to be sure. "You cut up your quilt?"

"I can always make another one. You need the cushioning." She took another section of quilt and stripped the batting off, then ripped the yellow calico into strips and dunked them into the plaster. "Hold your foot at a ninety-degree angle." Around and around his foot and ankle, halfway up his shin, she wrapped the strips. When she'd built a thick boot, she frosted it with more plaster. "Don't move. Not even your toes."

Vola left for the porch and came back with her arms full. She set two iron skillets on burners, flipped a hunk of butter into each, and turned on the flames. She cracked a couple of eggs into a yellow bowl and started whisking in milk, then cornmeal.

A cool breeze, fragrant with turned earth and frying butter, lifted against Peter. He looked at the sturdy cast drying, his foot safe inside now, wrapped in what used to be Vola's quilt. "I'm sorry. About how I've been." He tipped his head to her notice board.

"My philosophy bingo cards," she said with a nod. "No-bat Peter, those are just things I figure to be true about the world. The universals. The important ones are the things I figure out to be true about me. I keep them somewhere else, private."

125

"How come?"

"How come they're the important ones, or how come they're private?"

Peter shrugged. *Either. Both.* He leaned back, waiting.

Vola eyed him as she sawed a slice off a ham joint and forked it into one of the frying pans. She dipped out three ladles of batter, poured them sputtering into the other pan, then set the bowl down. "I'm going to tell you a story.

"When I got out of the service, I didn't remember a single true thing about myself. That's what training does. No more individuals, just pieces they can mould to their machine.

"I was lost my first day as a civilian. Lost. I went into a supermarket, I stared at all the choices, and I kept wondering who I was supposed to be buying groceries for. What filled this person's hungry belly? Gumbo or pie? Beans or bread? In the produce aisle, I broke down because I didn't remember a single thing about myself."

Vola went quiet then, her eyes closed.

"What happened?" Peter nudged after a moment.

"What happened?"

"In the store. What happened in the store?"

"Oh." She turned back to the stove and flipped the johnnycakes. "Peanut butter."

"Peanut butter *happened*?"

Vola tossed her hands into the air. "Peanut butter happened. And I was lucky it did. There I was on the floor of the supermarket – dirty, red-and-white-checked linoleum, I will never forget – weeping. And I knew I wouldn't get up until I remembered what kind of food I liked."

Vola stacked the johnnycakes on a blue plate, then paused. Peter thought she might be drifting back to the memory of that supermarket floor. He was glad he hadn't seen something like that – a grown woman, sobbing on a dirty supermarket floor. A crazy lady, with one lost leg. He felt suddenly protective and hoped no one had laughed at her, and that she had gotten herself out okay. "And . . ."

"Oh. And finally I did. I remembered my grandmother telling me that when I first discovered peanut butter sandwiches, I wanted one every day. So I got up from the floor and I bought myself some peanut butter and bread. I filled my cart with peanut butter and bread, because I decided I wasn't coming back until I knew for sure something else I liked to eat. And I was afraid that might be a long time."

She added the ham to the plate, slapped on a scoop of

applesauce, and brought it over to him along with a white jug of maple syrup. "Eat."

Peter flooded the plate with syrup and loaded a fork. The cornmeal had a gritty crunch; the ham was smooth and salty against the sweet syrup. It was the best food he could remember eating.

"And was it?" he asked when he'd cleaned half the plate. "A long time before you remembered something else?"

Vola pressed a finger to the drying cast. "Almost set. Keep still a while longer." She went back to the stove and carved more ham and ladled more batter into the skillet. "It was. People around me, they called it PTSD, post-traumatic stress disorder, from being in the war. And they were right that I was sick. But I knew it wasn't being in the war, exactly. It was that in the war, I had forgotten everything that was true about myself. Post-traumatic forgetting-who-you-are disorder, that's what I had.

"My grandfather was in a nursing home by then, and he was dying. I went out to his place – it had been my old home, too, my grandparents raised me for a couple of years – to clean it out.

"It was the end of summer. The orchard was an untended mess, but there were still some peaches hanging on. And that was the second lucky thing that happened to me, after the peanut butter. Because I suddenly remembered: Lord, I had loved those peaches. I used to sneak out in the middle of the night to pick them. I'd sprawl on the grass underneath those trees with fireflies flashing all around and katydids singing, a heap of peaches on my belly, and I'd eat them till the juice ran into my ears.

"I remembered that so clearly. I could smell that memory, I could hear it, and I could taste it. But I couldn't figure out how that girl could be the same person who had put on a uniform, picked up a gun, and done the things I did in the war. So I reached up and picked one of those peaches, and I laid myself down on the grass and bit into it, and . . . and there I was. I found another little true piece of my old self."

She brought the skillet over and stacked more johnnycakes and ham on to his empty plate, then went back to the stove.

"Stop," Peter said.

"Stop? Well, that's the end of the story anyway."

"No, I mean this'll be enough food. Thank you." Peter wished again that his fox were under the table, wondered again if Pax was hungry. And then had the curious sense

129

that he wasn't – that tonight, at least, Pax had food in his belly. "So then what?" he asked after loading his fork. "You were okay?"

Vola set the skillet in the sink and came back to sit across from him at the table. "What a person likes to eat? That's a detail. I was so lost, I needed to find out *all* the true things about myself. The little things to the biggest of all: what did I believe in at my core?"

Peter figured he knew what was coming. "Like war. Now you're anti-war, right?"

Vola steepled her fingers under her chin. "That's a complicated thing. What I am is *for* telling the truth about it. About what it costs. People should tell the truth about what war costs. That's taken me a long time to figure out." She leaned back. "And that was just one thing. I had to relearn everything that was right and wrong for me. But I couldn't – the world was too loud for me to hear myself think. So I moved into my grandfather's place. I decided to stay there until I knew who I was again."

Peter looked up at the jarred peaches on the shelf above him, then recalled the blooming trees in the orchard. "And you're still here," he said. "This is that place, isn't it?"

15

The sun burned through a dawn fog. The two foxes had been travelling for hours, but Grey was slow and rested often, so they had only just reached the valley basin. For the most part, Pax respectfully flanked the older fox, but sometimes he broke away to race at full speed for long glorious minutes before circling back.

He had never run before, not really. He'd sprinted around the borders of his pen or across the yard, but this running was a different thing: neat oval paws, healed now, skimming the ground only for traction as he galloped faster and faster over great sweeps of grass.

Yesterday's meal had cleared his senses and fuelled his muscles, but now the eggs were gone from his belly and the smells of the warming valley brought on a powerful hunger. Where the humans were, there would be food. *How far?*

Two days' travel. Grey described a place of old stone walls where the earth smelled faintly of tar and hemp, bordered by a river. *We will reach it by dusk. The human settlements are another day's travel beyond that.*

Pax did not remember human settlements. He did not remember a river. Of his home, he remembered the looming door. He remembered oaks ringing the house, the overgrown remains of a flower garden he was never allowed into, the sounds of a road. He sensed that other humans lived along this road, but he had never encountered them. These memories were fading, as was the memory of being caged. He could no longer recall what the sky looked like through hexagons of cage wire.

He remembered his boy, though. The hazel eyes with their odd round pupils; the way Peter would close them and throw his head back and yelp something near a bark when he was delighted. His salty neck that smelled sometimes of sweat and sometimes of soap. His hands, always moving, with their scent of chocolate, which Pax loved, and of mitt leather, which he loathed.

As the two foxes travelled on, Pax reflected on the puzzle of the other scent of his boy – his underlying scent. It hung between grief and yearning, and it welled from a deep ache for something that Pax could never divine.

Sometimes, in the boy's nest room, this grief-yearning scent was so strong that it overpowered everything else, and yet his boy made no move to acquire whatever it was he wanted so badly. Whenever Pax caught that scent, he would hurry from wherever he was to find Peter flung across his bed, clutching the objects he kept hidden in the bottom drawer of his bureau, his face set in hard ridges. Pax would nose Peter's shirtsleeve, or claw up the curtains, then pretend to lose his footing and fall to the floor – anything to get his boy to play. But when the grief-yearning scent was strongest, none of his tricks would work. On those days, Peter would shoo Pax outside and shut the door.

Remembering this, Pax felt the urge to run again, but not for the joy of it. *This war that is coming – are you sure it will harm all in its path? Even the youth?*

Everything. It will destroy everything.

Pax nosed Grey, respectful but urgent. They must hurry. The older fox studied the younger one for a moment, then began to trot. They crossed the marshy seam of the valley and climbed the rocky cliffs, shoulder to shoulder this time.

At the top of the rise, the two foxes stopped. Grey was panting hard. Ahead, the pines towered up, promising long, cool pools of shade. But the markings here were strong: the challenger hunted this territory, and the threat in his scent was unmistakable. And almost immediately the ground beat with the light staccato of paws tearing toward them. Pax and Grey had barely braced themselves when the tawny fox burst from the underbrush, lips curled in a snarl, tail lashing.

Pax shrank back, but Grey advanced calmly, his body lowered enough to declare non-aggression. *We are only passing through.*

The challenger ignored the peaceful greeting and sprang, hitting the old fox hard in the flank and pinning him down, then sank his teeth into Grey's thin neck.

At Grey's pain scream, Pax's guard hairs lifted and his heartbeat quickened. His muscles thrummed with a fury he'd known only once: in the early days with his humans, the father had raised a hand to the boy, and Pax had shot across the room without thought, small kit-teeth tearing fiercely through the man's trouser leg. Now, as it had then, his back arched and a low growl rumbled deep in his throat.

The challenger spun round in surprise, and Pax charged him headlong. They rolled, teeth clipping at tender ears, hind claws digging for purchase in soft belly fur. The yellow fox was more skilled, but Pax's fighting was fuelled by an instinct to protect. When his teeth found the other's throat, the challenger scrambled to his feet and backed off, whimpering.

Pax leaped in front of Grey, shielding him as he'd shielded his boy that long-ago time, lifted his chest, and growled a warning. The challenger slunk away.

Pax shook off the blood from a dozen superficial scratches and then cleaned Grey's wound. The puncture was deep. He urged Grey to go back.

No. I will travel.

The two padded steadily for an hour through light woods, Pax restraining himself to keep pace with the ailing Grey, relieved at least that they kept moving. But when a murder of crows landed in the bare arms of a pecan tree, Grey doubled back and sat down at its base, ears pricked up intently at the commotion.

Pax waited, not patiently. After a moment the old fox barked for him. *The war is moving closer.*

How do you know this?

The crows. Listen.

Pax cocked his head. More shrieking birds swept in, descending into the lower branches, then flapping up again to higher perches in a cyclone of distress. *They're upset.*

The crows hulked their shoulders, spiked their feathers, jerked and dipped their shrieking beaks. Their discord set Pax's nerves on edge. *There is disorder.*

He attended more carefully. What he sensed alarmed him. He tried to describe it: Air choked with death. Fire and smoke. Blood in a river, the river running red with it, the earth drowning in blood. Chaos. *Everything is broken. The fibres of the trees, the clouds, even the air is broken.*

Yes. War. Where?

Pax attuned himself once more. *West. Still distant, but nearing. And now a small group of war-sick has come from the south to meet it.*

From the south.

Pax paced while Grey struggled to his feet. He offered again to travel alone, and again Grey refused to turn back home. Again they set out, and again their pace was slower than Pax wanted. They stopped only for meals of grubs and berries, and whenever they did, Pax searched the air for any trace of his boy's scent, for the faintest sound of his voice. None. None.

He lifted his muzzle and bayed a single aching note.

It had been so long since he'd seen his boy. Before this, they'd never been apart for more than half a day. Often, Peter would leave in the morning, and Pax would pace his pen in increasing distress until the afternoon, when Peter would come home, smelling of other young humans and of the strange breath of the large yellow bus that delivered him. With the afternoon, Pax could reassure himself his boy was all right, examining him for any sign of injury before he could relax into play.

It was afternoon now. He bayed again, and this time Grey lifted his voice in an echo of loss. But when Pax trotted back to the path to resume the journey, Grey faltered.

Pax could see that he needed rest. He led the wounded

fox to a mossy circle of shade beneath a pine. Grey laid his cheek on his paws, and before Pax had even finished cleaning his wound again, he was asleep.

As Pax kept watch, he thought of doing favourite things with his boy when he found him: tumbling together outside, playing hunting games, exploring the grassed yard and the bit of woods behind it. He remembered the ways his boy would reward him: the full smiles of greeting; the thorough neck scratchings, Peter's fingers digging in just hard enough. He recalled the peace of lying at his boy's feet in front of the fire.

These thoughts calmed Pax and he dozed with the memory of Peter's knuckles kneading the loose skin between his shoulder blades so real that his fur ruffled under it. Until a shifting breeze brought a scent that called him to instant alert.

Meat. Roasted meat, the kind his humans sometimes cooked over a fire in the yard. His boy would feed him bites of this meat, dripping with fat. For days afterward, Pax would scour the ashy fire bed for overlooked scraps. Even the charred bones were treasures.

Pax got to his paws to sniff more deeply. Yes, roasted meat. He nosed the sleeping Grey. *Humans are near.*

Grey moved more easily after his rest, and the two foxes kept up a loping pace. As they got closer, though, Pax charged ahead. His body was light, the fat burned off from days of scarce food. He ran as foxes are meant to run – compact body arrowing through the air at a swiftness that rippled his fur. The new joy of speed, the urgency of coming night, the hope of reunion with his boy – these things transformed him into something that shot like liquid fire between the trees. Something gravity couldn't touch. Pax could have run forever.

Until he galloped out from the woods and saw ahead of him a wide river. Beyond that stretched a clear field, flat and then rising up to massive crumbling stone walls. It was dusk now, and at the far corner of the stone ruins a dozen men were gathered around a fire, eating. Beyond them were a cluster of tents and several large vehicles.

The wind had shifted to the east. The grilled meat smoke still hung heavy in the air, but Pax could only get a general scent of the humans. He bounded up and down the river's edge, frustrated, but from no direction could he differentiate one human scent from another.

At least Pax knew his boy was not here. None of the humans had his reedy form, none moved with the same quick energy, none held himself as Peter had – upright, but with a downward cant of his head. He was relieved; the other scents of the encampment – smoke, diesel, scorched metal, and a strange, dark electrical odour – were things he would have herded Peter away from.

Grey limped from the woods and flopped to the riverbank beside Pax. Together, the two foxes watched the men. They had finished eating, but they remained around the fire, talking and laughing.

They are war-sick? Pax wanted to know.

Not now. They are peaceful now. I remember this peace. The old fox curled his forelegs under his chest. *At the end of the day, the humans I lived with gathered like those across the river.*

Suddenly Pax remembered: he had seen something similar as well. It hadn't happened for several years, but sometimes at the end of the day, his humans would sit together on his boy's nest. The father would lay a hard box, flat and thin and made of many layers of paper, across his lap. Paper, like Pax's own bedding, but not shredded, and with many marks. His humans would peel these layers, one by one, and study them. Pax remembered that his humans were most linked together on those evenings, and with their harmony he could let down his guard.

Pax felt a strange sensation – as if his chest were no longer large enough for his heart.

The foxes turned back to the men. Some were still crouched around the fire, while others moved with lanterns between the equipment and the tents. With full darkness, the remaining men rose from the fireside. They dumped out mugs of coffee, scuffed dirt over flames, and ducked into tents.

Grey rose also and limped uphill to the protection of a sweeping hemlock bough. He circled and curled himself up on the pine-needled ground underneath, his nose tucked under his brush.

The smell of the meat had made Pax too hungry to rest. He trotted to the edge of the river. Its current was soft. He dipped his head and drank and then jumped to a rock, slippery with moss but stable. Then, gaze fixed on the glow of the dying embers, he chose. A leap, a splash, and again his body did what it had never done before but was meant to do all along: he swam. A moment later, he climbed the bank and shook himself off.

Neither movement nor sound came from the tents. Pax crept silently across the field and climbed the rise. He circled the bounds of the camp, edging closer and closer to the fire bed.

The sense of danger was strong. It was hard not to flee. He was, after all, accustomed only to his two humans – the one he loved, the one he tolerated. Several times he crept to the very rim of the fire bed, found the smell of meat laced with the warning scent of the war-sick men, then leaped back.

A discarded pork bone, still redolent with fat, proved too much to resist. Pax darted in. As he gulped the meat, ash-gritted but still warm, the rustle of canvas startled him. He froze.

A man emerged from a tent. Silhouetted by lantern light, he stretched, and a long shadow snaked out to cloak the watching fox. The man turned away and relieved himself on a bush. The scent of his urine travelled to Pax, and he bristled to sharp alert:

His boy's father.

16

"That's enough."

The words, along with Vola's hand on Peter's shoulder, were a welcome relief. His foot throbbed, his shoulders ached, and his armpits were so chafed that they were bleeding. Two days of Boot Camp Vola – the secret name he'd christened the torture sessions in which he crutched uphill, dragged himself over stony ground on his elbows, and pitched mountains of hay balanced on one foot – had worn him out. He swung round to face the cabin, suddenly not even sure he could make it that far.

But above the roof of the cabin, the hills were veiled with rain clouds. Night was coming. He thought of Pax, wet and cold. "I could keep going."

"No. You'll undo the good if you push too fast."

Peter nodded and took a step toward the cabin.

But Vola shook her head. "Not yet." She pointed to the barn. "The third condition."

The barn seemed impossibly far away. Peter looked back at the cabin. He wanted to fall into that hammock. He planted his crutch tips in a deliberate show. "What is it?"

"Nothing much. You're going to work some puppets for me. Marionettes. That sound too hard?"

"Marionettes? I don't get it."

"You know what they are?"

"Sure." He pictured the only ones he'd seen up close: Punch and Judy characters with long chins and sharp noses, at a street fair when he'd been a little kid. Dead-eyed and skeletony as starving rats. The puppeteer had jerked them across the stage in twitchy rushes that had left him with nightmares for weeks. "What about them?"

Vola eyed him for a moment before answering. "Another true piece of myself I recovered: I remembered that I'd made some marionettes for my little nieces when

I was a teenager. I remembered how much I loved carving the wood."

She pulled two scarves from her overalls and handed them over with a sigh. "Wrap those handgrips. You're still hanging off the crutches. Take the weight on your palms, child. Spread it to your arms, even when you're just standing there."

Vola's unexpected kindnesses undid Peter. One minute she'd be barking at him for a dozen pull-ups, or shooting her fingers at his face, warning him not to get too close. It was comfortable that way. Like home. But the next minute she'd rub her salve into his aching shoulders, or sand the splinters off his crutches, or drop her chores to fix him a mug of hot chocolate, and he'd realise how much care she was putting into making him strong and mobile, and he felt guilty.

He felt guilty now, winding the soft cloth around the handgrips, so he told her what he figured she wanted to hear. "Your nieces must have been really happy to get such great presents." But he doubted it. Those nieces of hers had probably stuffed those rat-skeletony, dead-eyed puppets right into the bin the first night they'd gotten them. No bad dreams.

Vola shrugged, but Peter could tell she was secretly pleased by his words, and his guilt eased. He arranged his weight on his sore palms and followed her to the barn. In the doorway, he paused to draw in the cool air – it smelled of wood and hay and linseed oil and varnish. All good scents, Peter thought, separating them out. And really good together. He swung inside.

Vola crossed to the opposite wall, the one draped in burlap. Peter hung back. That wall had unnerved him the first day. She pulled the material aside and he nearly lost his balance, as though what he saw had hit him with a physical force. The puppets – marionettes, he could see now that they were marionettes hanging off the wall – were spookily realistic, and yet like nothing he'd ever seen.

He stepped closer and found his voice.

"Their eyes."

"My grandmother's jewellery. She had long jet neck-laces. The pupils are filled with those beads. They flash in the light, make my friends seem alive."

Peter fell silent again, and Vola didn't disturb him as he studied the creatures hanging in front of him.

Five were human – a king and a queen, a child, a pirate or sailor, and a sorceress – the rest animals. All the heads were wooden, nearly human sized and huge eyed, but the bodies were of a wild variety of materials. A tortoise was shelled with a green and orange gourd. Pinecone bracts formed a serpent's scales. And feathers: almost all the puppets wore an assortment of feathers as hair or headdresses, or cloaks or breeches. Looped neatly over pegs beside each marionette was an array of dowels and paddles, strung together with thin black cord.

In the centre of the wall hung what Peter guessed was the largest puppet, covered by a separate piece of cloth. Vola removed it and he gasped.

The great bird's wings were magnificent, probably a good five feet at full span. Hundreds of dark feathers gracefully overlapped each other in perfect rows, the tips painted red, as if licked with fire. Vola lifted it from its perch and carried it over to Peter. "Most of the others are head and shoulder puppets, but this one needs to fly. I jointed him at the elbow. When he soars, you can almost feel the wind. Go ahead: you can touch him."

Peter reached out. His fingertips stroked a sleek feathered shoulder, then the sharp wooden beak, painted a bright gold. The bird's eyes glittered huge and black. He dropped his hand. "So what do I have to do with this?"

Vola motioned to the hay bales. "May as well sit down. I'm going to begin at the beginning."

Peter sank on to a bale of hay, grateful for the rest. He watched as Vola hung the great bird back up. She pulled a small book from a niche in the wall, then came and sat beside Peter with it cradled in her hands. "I killed someone."

She looked up. Peter wasn't quick enough to cover his shock.

She heaved a sigh, thick with disgust. "No matter what *dyableman* lines they feed you about learning trades and reaching your potential, you're there to kill people. Kill or be killed – that's the contract in war."

That wasn't true. His father, for example. "You won't be fighting, right?" Peter had pressed. His father had laughed and said no, he'd just be doing pretty much what he did as a civilian: laying wires.

Peter didn't bother correcting Vola, though, because the look on her face was so wrecked. "You killed someone."

"I probably killed a lot of people, or at least contributed to their deaths. But this one . . . this one I saw. After. I had to search his body. We were trained to look for weapons, anything we could use.

"I dropped to my knees. I had to touch him, looking for those weapons. I remember being shocked at the feel of him – I was a medic, but still I half expected him to be plastic, not real. The way they taught us to think of the enemy in our training. But, of course, he was . . . he was warm. It was cold out, and he was giving off warmth. As if his life was steaming out of him. And I was touching him without his permission. I'd murdered him, but what bothered me was that he had lost the right to say yes or no about what happened to him. You probably think that's crazy, don't you?"

Peter's mouth had gone dry. He didn't know what to say. And then suddenly he thought of the kind-eyed therapist, and he did know. "That must have been hard for you."

Vola looked at him with a surprised relief on her face. She nodded. "Suddenly, I was desperate to know who he was. Where he'd come from, what he cared about, who loved him. His mouth was open, as if he might have wanted to speak to me. I realised something then: that even though he was a man, even though he was a different race, even though he had grown up in a different country – we might have had a lot in common. Important things, more important than which army had drafted us. Two but not two. But I'd killed him, so now we would never know. I searched his body, not for weapons but for clues to who he'd been." Vola went silent, her face so devastated that Peter wanted to look away.

"And . . ."

"And this." Vola lifted the book. "*The Seven Voyages of Sinbad*. Part of the Arabian Nights series, in his pocket. He'd carried it into war, so it had to have meant something. An old copy, so probably it had been his favorite as a boy. Sinbad was brave, so maybe he thought it brought him courage. Or maybe he just wanted to remember that once he had been a little boy, and he had read books and felt safe. A page was bookmarked: the story of how Sinbad escapes from the Roc's nest. I figured that story helped him believe that one day he'd escape, too, and get back home."

Vola got up. She lifted the great winged puppet off the wall again. "The Roc. This bird could snatch up elephants in its talons. Look at it." She carried the bird back to Peter and turned its beak to face him.

Its gaze was so fierce that Peter shrank back. "What do I have to do with this?" he asked again.

"That book was so important to that soldier that he'd carried it to war. I figured since I'd taken his life, I owed him something. I owed it to him to tell the story that meant so much to him. I carved all these puppets, and I've been telling the story of Sinbad escaping from the Roc here in my barn for nearly twenty years." Vola handed the control apparatus to Peter. "And now, finally, I'm going to get to see what it looks like."

17

*P*ax watched Grey lap at the river's edge, *then stumble* back. For two days now, the foxes had rested across from the war-sick camp, but Grey had not gotten better. When the old fox reached the spicy shade of the hemlock bough, he collapsed. His eyes were hollow and glazed, and he barely flinched when Pax cleaned his neck once more.

Pax found the wound even more inflamed. *Stay hidden. Rest.*

He left Grey and climbed upstream to a place he'd discovered where the river narrowed beside a gorge wall and the underbrush beside it was dense enough that he could move about unseen by the humans. He'd had little luck hunting – the area was teeming with mice and rabbits, but they scampered from Pax's clumsy attempts to catch them. Besides beetles and unripe berries, he'd been able to swipe only a few crayfish, which Grey had refused.

For half an hour, Pax tried – he chased scurrying voles and hopping wrens, and once a sunning frog. But each time he sprang, his jaws snapped around only air. He grew hungrier with each failure. He wanted meat – for himself and for his weakened companion. The rich smells from the camp tormented him.

He leaped into the water. The current was swift there, but midway across, three boulders rested against one another to form a secure perch. From there, Pax had a clear view downstream to the humans.

More had come. A few were women; most were men. Pax checked for his boy constantly because the father was still here and because he sensed that his home was not far away, but only full-grown humans appeared.

Many of them were in the field now. Some were down near the riverbank unrolling wires directly across from Grey, which made Pax uneasy. But the soldiers did not seem interested in anything except their labour.

Pax had learned their routine. Each morning, two of them entered the tent that his senses told him was full of food. Then these two would cook at the fire, and the other war-sick would gather to eat. Afterward, they all toiled – in the field, in the vehicles, unloading more and more machinery – but no one went near the grub tent until dusk, when the same two would cook the evening food, then call the others to gather.

It was mid-afternoon. Pax watched for a while longer to be certain the war-sick were occupied, then crossed over the remaining span of rushing water along a fallen tree. Belly to the ground, he made his way across the ridge to a spot above the old mill.

There he paused to survey the scene. Three men were positioned at the encampment just below him. They huddled over new equipment on the south edge of the mill, where two thick walls met.

The rest of the humans were in the field. Some rolled spools of wire to the holes they'd dug near the riverbank. Others lowered boxes into those holes, then shovelled dirt over them.

Two pairs had crossed the river. They were digging holes on the far bank, some directly below the hemlock where Grey was resting. Pax knew that the humans would not scent Grey, and that Grey would not venture out while they were near. Still, he bristled in anxiety. He would move the wounded fox to a safer place tonight.

Pax darted to the north edge of the mill ruins, near the tents and vehicles. There, a birch tree angled out from the stone wall.

Pax stopped short.

He had been here before. This place – the tree with its peeling white bark, the walls, the field below scented with wild onions and timothy grass and the faintest odour of tar – he recognised them all. He'd been here with his boy long ago, as a kit.

The scene returned. Sticks. Peter and three other boys had rushed each other from these stone walls, whooping and brandishing sticks. They'd been laughing, but those swinging sticks had made Pax uneasy. He'd shadowed Peter, yipping at the other boys when they came too near, until Peter had tied him to this very tree. Pax had whined and chewed at the rope the rest of the afternoon.

Peter had been here! Pax sniffed the tree and the base of the wall thoroughly, but he could find no trace of his boy now. The war-sick men, though – their scent was everywhere, strong and dangerous. Pax's gut tightened.

He checked the tents until he was certain there was no movement around them. Then he made a dash for the grub tent. At the corner he paused, checked again, and then slipped under a flap.

Inside, meat hung above tables heaped with onions and potatoes – a bonanza for his taking. Pax sprang and seized a joint of ham, tearing it from its hook, and darted out of the tent with the heavy prize in his mouth.

He ran hard uphill, behind the walls and back through the shrubby wood. At the river, he dropped the ham and gulped down a meal of the salty meat. He tore the joint apart and buried two large hunks in the sandy soil at the river's edge, and then marked the caches.

He picked up the remaining piece, lush with meat and fat that would nourish Grey for days, and carried it over the fallen trunk. He paused on the pile of boulders to survey the camp again.

The humans had disappeared. A new odour, faint but menacing, hung in the air. Pax recognised it. When he was a yearling, the father had brought a fan to his boy's room. Pax had hated the dark electrical scent coming off the wire between the fan and the wall. One night, when the odour was especially dangerous, Pax had chewed through the wire, as if killing a snake.

Pax's every instinct urged him to run from the menacing scent, but he would not leave without Grey. And just then he saw the old fox stagger out from beneath the hemlock bough, making his way back to the river.

Grey tripped. Instantly, the scorched-air smell sizzled up from the spot like an earthborn bolt of lightning, and at the same second the riverbank exploded. Soil and rock and river and turf blew up in a furious roar, then fell back to the cratered earth like harsh black rain.

Pax dropped the ham and barked for Grey. His ears rang in a shuddering silence.

The war-sick poured out from behind the walls. From their cries, Pax knew they were excited. They ran down the field, splashed across the river, and spread out over the smoking bank. After several moments of searching, they made their way back to the camp.

When the last of the war-sick had returned, Pax tore down the gorge.

The great hemlock bough lay across Grey's chest, cleaved from the tree. Pax nosed his friend's muddy cheek, pawed his flank. He sniffed Grey's muzzle. There was breath there, but just barely.

Pax lay down shoulder to shoulder with the old fox, pressing tight in full company. He could offer only withness, but nothing else was asked.

Linked with Grey's final memories, he heard the song of an arctic bird instead of the humans' shouts. Instead of the ashy haze that hung over them, he saw with Grey a vast blue bowl of sky. Instead of lying on gritted ground, he tumbled with Grey and his brother kits across a snowy tundra spiked with starry blue flowers. He purred with Grey under his silver mother's rough tongue, tasted her warm milk, felt the weight of her chin resting over his newborn skull. And then peace.

The old fox was still.

Pax rose. He pressed his forehead into his friend's cheek. He reared back and bayed, heedless of whether the war-sick heard. And then he ran.

There was no joy in the running this time, but there was relief that his body served him. He ran and he ran, north through the dusk, north through the night.

As dawn crested, he entered the challenger's territory, and still he ran. The yellow fox charged out to face him, but fell back from the determination of Pax's course and let him pass. Pax galloped down the cliff, tore across the valley bottom, and strained up the final long rise to the meadow. Midway, he stopped and lifted his head.

Three foxes watched him approach. They were familiar to him now: Grey's mate, still big-bellied with kits; Runt, half her size, nearby.

Bristle did not stand with them. Her bright fur shone at the base of the large pine that towered over the meadow, the pine under which her sister had died.

The scent of Grey's death was on Pax's fur, but the foxes knew already.

Pax padded up the rest of the way. When he reached Grey's den, he lifted his head and wailed the notes of grief. Three foxes answered in kind.

Grey's mate approached. She sniffed Pax's nose and then his flank. She learned of the fight, which did not kill her mate, and of the humans' explosion, which did. She learned also that Pax had protected Grey, had fed him, had cleaned his wounds, for which she was grateful. And then she learned the news Grey had died trying to obtain.

It is not safe for us in the south?

It is not safe.

Grey's mate walked away, her belly swaying.

His message delivered, Pax dropped to the grass, exhausted. Runt came to claim the space beside him, and

Pax was glad to allow the little fox to groom him. Bristle watched from the base of the pine above them.

Pax slept fitfully through the afternoon, plagued by dreams in which his boy was tangled in smoking wires. Finally, as the moon rose in an indigo sky, he got to his feet.

He breathed the scents of the foxes, linked in grief over the loss of their silver centre. He was linked to them by the same grief, and he knew he would be welcomed in this valley if he chose to stay. But his dreams urged him back to the war-sick camp.

As he was about to leave, he sensed Bristle tearing down the hill. He waited.

Where are you going?

Pax shared his new understanding that the exploding earth was war, and that the wires caused death. He shared his fear that his boy might come upon them if he joined his father, and his determination to protect Peter.

These explosions – they would kill humans?

Yes.

She sprang round to face him. *Then leave them.*

Pax ignored her. He gathered himself and leaped. He hit the ground at a run.

18

*P*eter dropped from the beam when he caught sight of Vola limping through the rain toward the barn, and tried not to look guilty. Vola was suspicious he'd been doing more than the exercises she'd ordered – he was, doubling them usually – and she wasn't happy about it. "It takes a healthy adult four weeks to do what you're trying to do in one. You're bound to hurt yourself," she'd warned him several times. In just these few days it had become an old argument.

He watched her shake off water in the doorway and it reminded him of Pax, the dog-like way he did that. Was it raining where he was? Would he still shake himself off if there was no warm, dry inside to come into? Peter shivered and rubbed his arms.

"What's the matter? You look like you're in pain. Your arms hurt?"

"No." Of course they did. But it was a good hurt, a soreness that meant he was getting closer to being strong enough to go. He dropped and did three push-ups, his cast resting on his left ankle. "See? Fine. Can I do the obstacle course now? It's not raining as hard."

"No. You can't get the cast wet. I'll figure out some way to waterproof it before you leave, but for today, stay in here. You do all your drills already?"

"Beam work, sack dragging, cinder blocks. All that core work you taught me."

Vola nodded to the wall of marionettes. "Why don't you practice, then?"

Because those puppets don't get me a minute closer to my fox, Peter wanted to say. He sighed deeply and rolled his eyes instead.

Vola was unmoved. "How are you coming with them?"

"Okay. Good, I mean." He'd practiced a few times. And gotten a little better. The strings didn't tangle up, anyway. Sometimes, though, the controls still worked exactly the opposite of the way he expected them to, and the puppets always looked twitchy, as if they were being electrocuted. But he had run out of patience.

"Let's do the show. I'm going to be leaving soon, Vola." Peter lifted the crutches, which moved as if they were extensions of his arms now. "I made it to the ridge and back twice yesterday – I was on these things almost six hours. I would have done eight except you took them away, remember? I'm ready to go."

Vola dropped a handful of nails into an overall pocket and slid a hammer into her belt loop. Then she levelled him a gaze. "Show me how you work Sinbad."

Peter gave another sigh, which Vola ignored again, and picked Sinbad off the wall. He swept the puppet over a bale of hay and dropped it on to the wooden egg in the big tin bowl that Vola had painted to look like a nest. He knew how clumsy it looked, but he sent her a hopeful glance.

"Really? That's the desperate hero, risking his life for a chance to escape the mighty Roc?"

Vola took the controls from him, and instantly the marionette seemed to become flesh and blood. "Think about what he wants: to escape," she said, as if Peter had

asked for a lesson. "Drop his arms and lead with them, like this, see, kind of low and sneaky. Have him sink down into the nest till he's hidden behind the egg. Once he's there, you can let him go and fly the Roc over the nest from the other side – from the right, remember, so it doesn't tangle Sinbad's strings. Bring it down directly on to the egg, nice and slow, so the magnets in its talons catch hold of the ones in Sinbad's hands."

"They don't move like that for me. Why don't you just set up a mirror and watch yourself act it out?"

Vola glared at him. "It's the third condition, and it's not optional. Come over here." She carried the puppet to her workbench.

"He wants to move. All the puppets *want* to move because I made them that way. You just have to show them how. Your muscles to theirs, your muscles to theirs."

She took off Sinbad's cloak. Then, to Peter's shock, she unstrung his wires. She reached for a screwdriver and disassembled the puppet until he was nothing more than a pile of scattered parts. Then she held the screwdriver out.

Peter clamped the crutches under his armpits and raised his palms.

"You watched, didn't you?"

"Yes, but—"

"I just stopped in for some tools. I'll be back in an hour. You'll have this puppet put together again, and you won't have any more problems after that." She slapped the screwdriver into his hand and left without another word.

It wasn't actually that hard. The marionette's knees and elbows were simple one-way hinges, the shoulders and hips carved wooden ball joints, which Peter could see allowed for greater movement. The hands and feet were fastened with leather straps.

The stringing was trickier. But once he figured out that the hands had to work off the control that moved like a dragonfly, he was able to figure out the others.

And Vola was right: after he'd refastened Sinbad, he could move the puppet more smoothly. "Your muscles to theirs," Vola had said, and sure enough, Peter was able to translate the movements she'd suggested through his own body to Sinbad's.

"Your muscles to theirs" didn't work for the Roc. Peter flexed his shoulders, swooped his arms, but the bird only lurched a few strokes and then fell as if it had been shot. The bird's glittering gaze seemed a reproach.

"I'm sorry, bird. I don't know what you're supposed to be doing, though. Are you trying to eat the guy? Are you protecting your egg?"

Suddenly Peter wanted to know the Roc's story, wanted to get it right. He found the slot where Vola kept the Sinbad book. As he drew it out, he heard a quiet thunk. There was something at the back of the niche.

He pulled it out. A square tin, faded yellow and decorated with the peeling words SUNSHINE BISCUITS. He steadied it on his palm and thought back to the battered cookie tin he'd found at his grandfather's, the one with its heap of soldiers guarding the surprising photo.

He pried off the lid. Inside was a stack of index cards, scrawled with handwriting he'd already come to recognise. He knew instantly that he held in his hand Vola's personal truths, the ones she kept hidden. He snapped down the lid, not wanting to invade her privacy. But it was too late – he'd read the top one:

I would have been a good teacher.

It wasn't a terrible truth, and it didn't even seem all that personal. Still, he wished he hadn't seen it. He pushed the tin back into the niche and slid the book in after it just as Vola came back in.

He pointed to the marionettes. "I've got it now. Let's do the scene."

But Vola only walked to her workbench and poured oil on to a whetstone. "Not yet. We need a stage first. I'll put something together when I've got some free time."

"A stage? You didn't say anything about a stage!"

"The marionettes don't just swing around in thin air over a couple of hay bales." She turned round and raised a palm to cut off Peter's protest. "Listen, boy, I will see that soldier's story the way it should be seen. You'll have to respect how much that means to me even if you don't understand it. Which you should, by the way. You carrying that charm around – it's the same thing. You're telling that story of your mother's for her."

"But it will take so long . . ."

"And there's no hurry – you're going to be here another week anyway." She clumped back to the workbench, sat down hard, and began selecting tools. Discussion over.

Peter flung himself on to a stack of hay bales. Another week of this and he'd go crazy.

The word struck him. He didn't think of Vola as crazy any more. He propped himself on his elbows and studied her as she polished her tools, noticing how carefully she lifted and cleaned each one. How, when she finished, she laid it precisely in its place. There was a calm purposefulness to her movements that he liked. A predictability.

François waddled in and yawned. He climbed to a crotch in the rafters above the workbench and started washing himself before a nap. It occurred to Peter that, like François, he'd grown comfortable with Vola.

Peter craned his head to see what she was making. A handle. She'd brought in a broken hoe, and she was giving it a new handle. A simple thing, and yet it struck him as almost magic. Like his crutches. Before he'd had them, he'd been helpless. Vola had nailed a couple of boards together, and now he could swing over miles of rough country, quick and sure. Magic.

He pulled the crutches over and braced them under his arms, feeling the familiar comfort their sturdy strength brought. He swung over to the workbench. "I want to make something. Will you show me?"

Vola leaned back to study him hard. After what seemed a full minute, she nodded. "No sense letting your brain go to rot. You know anything at all about working with wood?"

"'Carve away from yourself' – I know that much."

"That's a start. But that's not what I meant." Vola chose a fresh block from her wood bin and centred it on the workbench. "Who is the master here?"

"Excuse me?"

"Who is the boss: me or the wood?"

Peter understood that this was a test. He looked at the wood, blank and still, waiting. Then he looked at the neat arcs of gleaming tools, so eager to cut, they seemed to tremble. "You. You're the master."

Vola nodded. She selected a spoon-tipped chisel and a mallet, then gave the block the same searching look she'd given him a few minutes ago – as if she were trying to read some secret message below its surface. She tapped the chisel into the fresh wood. It cut with a clean snap, and a curled chip flipped on to the bench.

She turned to Peter. "And now? Who is the master now?"

Vola's face told him nothing. But the wood, its missing wedge now a question demanding a response, spoke. "The wood is," he said, certain.

"That's right," Vola agreed. "From this moment on, the wood is the master. The carver is servant to the wood. All craftsmen are servants to the craft. Once you decide

171

what you want to make, the project is the boss. You know what you want to make?"

The answer came right away. "How do you carve a fox?"

As soon as the words left his mouth, Peter braced for the answer he figured was coming – about how he should figure it out for himself. But Vola surprised him.

"Michelangelo was once asked how he'd created one of his statues. He said, 'I saw the angel in the marble and carved until I set him free.' Might be a good way to think about it. Of course, if you're going to try to find the fox in the wood, you'll have to start with some wood."

She motioned Peter to follow her to the wood bin. "Different woods, different merits. Basswood's easy to carve, holds fine detail, and it's light. I use it for the marionettes' heads. Now, this pine—"

"White ash is good for baseball bats," Peter offered. "It's really hard."

Vola passed the pine block from one hand to the other in silence for a moment. "Speaking of which . . ." She turned to Peter. "You really don't own a bat? You love baseball, but don't own a bat?"

"I'm a fielder."

"So . . . what? You wait for someone to hit the ball,

then you go get it? That's just reacting. Don't you want to hit, too?"

"That's not how it is. Once I've got the ball, I'm in control. I'm not reacting; I'm making choices. And I hit. The team has bats. You don't know baseball."

"Maybe I don't know baseball." She tossed the wood back into the bin with a shrug. "But I'm starting to know you. And I think you need yourself a bat."

Peter turned to the bin. He ran his hand through the blocks of wood while the image of blue glass shattering over white roses swept him. The image he could avoid when he stood at the plate, a team bat in hand, only by aiming his fiercest concentration on the pitcher's moves.

If he owned his own bat again, every time he picked it up, he would see that shattered blue glass over those white roses. And it would wreck him.

He lifted a honey-coloured piece of wood, just the size Pax had been when he'd found him. "How about this?" he asked, his breathing tight. "It's rippled, like fur."

Vola looked as if she was biting her lip against more of the bat debate. "Butternut," she said finally. "Beautiful grain. Soft enough. You study it for a while. We'll carve tomorrow."

Late that night, as he was about to climb into his hammock bone weary, Peter saw the block of wood he'd propped on the windowsill earlier. He'd barely thought about Pax all day. Guilt swept him. He was becoming foxless, something he hadn't been since he was seven years old.

It had taken a lot longer – a year and sixteen days to be exact, he'd figured it out – for a day to go by when he didn't think about his mother. On that day, he'd gone with a friend's family on a camping trip. They'd gotten into canoes in the morning, and fished and swum and pitched tents and grilled hot dogs. Only when he climbed into his sleeping bag under the stars had his disloyalty struck him. He'd worried that night that he deserved to be motherless.

He pulled her picture out from his pack. Her birthday, the kite. One of the very good memories. The kite hadn't flown – he'd been six years old, and really it wasn't anything more than a picture of a dragon taped to some Popsicle sticks. Even at that age, he'd known that if his father had been there, somehow the kite's failure would have ruined the afternoon. But he wasn't there, and his mother had just laughed about it, and they'd spread a blanket on the hill and made a picnic of peanut brittle and grape juice and made up story after story about that paper dragon who was too wise to go flying off into the air when so many other adventures were waiting for him on the ground.

Peter set the photo on the sill beside the block of wood. He closed his eyes. He needed to visit some memories of Pax, too.

Pax, waiting at the door of his pen whenever Peter got home because he'd learned the whine of the school-bus brakes. Nosing through his rucksack for apple cores. Peeking out of his sweatshirt pocket. Peter had snuck him into school once – in second grade, he hadn't thought of the consequences to the kit, but had only wanted the secret comfort of his company. There'd been a fire drill, and the alarm had terrified Pax. Peter had been sent home and his father had been angry, but the way the kit had shivered and mewed had been the true punishment.

The best memory was a quiet one. The winter before last had been cold, with long stretches when Peter hadn't wanted to leave the fireplace to do his homework. It had been so cold that his father had relented and allowed Pax inside early to stretch out close to the fire. Pax would doze with his muzzle and front paws getting so hot that Peter kept checking them. Peter remembered his knuckles drifting down as he read his history text to knead the fur between his pet's shoulder blades. Peace.

He opened his eyes and lifted the butternut block. And in the pale light of the moon, he saw the fox in the wood.

19

*B*ristle had started out after Pax, but his long bounds had outpaced hers and he had run hard all through the night, all through the morning. He had not sensed her presence for hours when he reached the river in front of the mill in the afternoon. He slipped silently into a stand of green reeds, downstream from where Grey's body rested. He dipped his head to drink. When his thirst was slaked, he pushed the reeds aside.

The field was empty. The vehicles were gone. There was no sign of the humans, but their scents were fresh and even sharper than before. They were nearby, and they were anxious. Pax climbed upstream and crossed the river at the narrows, then hurried along the treed ridge to observe the site from above.

New gouges raked across the hillside behind the mill ruins. Like a skulk of foxes taking to its dens, the soldiers had retreated to their trenches: a few still digging, others working on equipment, still others talking together over charts. The vehicles rested behind the walls also.

Pax retraced his steps back along the ridge, back across the river, back downstream. Again he slipped into the reeds, and looking up from there, he saw no humans this time either. The dark electric scent hung heavy in the air.

The wind eddied, bearing smoke from the west. He'd smelled it twice on his way, but now it was thicker, more dangerous. Closer.

Pax could not wait until the safety of night.

He dived into the water and swam with only his sleek head above its surface, climbed the bank, and shook the water from his fur. Keeping low, he headed for the closest cover – a scrub oak skirted with new suckers at its base, just a few full-bounds away.

From there, he sighted the advantage he needed: midway down from the mill walls, where the field began to flatten out, a purple granite slab shouldered out of the ground. A bundle of wires trailed over this outcrop before dropping back into the grass.

Pax crept out. His paws sensed a threat from the ground: more boxes were buried near the bank, the field crossed with more wires. Leaping clear of the wires, he skimmed the grasses so swiftly that they barely parted.

At the base of the slab he flattened himself and perked his ears uphill. By the steady rhythms of their voices and tools, he knew that the soldiers had not moved from the trenches. The breeze was still downhill – it would alert him if they approached.

He pulled a wire out and began to gnaw at it. Before he'd chewed through the sheathing, a fury of teeth attacked him from behind. He hit the rock hard, the wind knocked out of him. He rolled to his feet and saw Bristle leap over him to the crest of the slab.

From that height, she held the advantage. *The crows say war-sick humans are nearing. This exploding earth, these death wires, leave this for them to find.*

Pax was larger than Bristle, but he was no match for her determination. Every time he attempted to reclaim his position at the wire, her snapping jaws held him away.

He circled the outcrop, climbing closer to the mill than he liked, to come at her from above. But before he could pounce, a movement down at the river caught his eye.

Bristle noted his alarm but kept her gaze locked on Pax. *The humans have arrived?*

Pax sensed an eager thrill below the question. *No. Another fox, I think.*

Bristle refused to be distracted. *No fox from our valley would venture past the territory boundary.*

Pax rose on his haunches for a clearer view. He saw it again – a narrow copper wedge, tipped with white, that rose and disappeared, rose and disappeared, running beside the riverbank along exactly the path he had taken earlier, the same path Bristle must have tracked to find him.

At the reeds, another red flash. A small fox splashed into the water. And Pax recognised him.

He shrieked a warning.

Bristle turned to look then. Runt struggled out of the water beside the scrub oak. Instantly Bristle sprang up, seeming to double in size. In a single leap she cleared the ledge and then flew down the slope.

No, back! Home! Back! She flashed through the

grasses. The panic in her voice only seemed to spur Runt on – he rose again to get her position and then loped in joyful bounds toward her.

Pax pounced on the wire, but he was too late.

Just as he stripped off its sheathing, a dark odour of lightning blew through the earth. A jolt of current shattered one of his back teeth. It seared his bottom lip, scorched his throat, and sizzled down his spine.

And then a swath of lower field exploded into the sky. Pax was knocked off the ledge, and when he hit solid ground again, tangled in uprooted shrubbery, the broken world went silent. His skull rang in the silence, and he watched shock-still as the storm of hot dirt and rocks and branches and weeds rained down upon him and then wasted itself to a veil of grit.

He staggered to his feet and sucked the burned air into his flattened lungs until his head cleared. Then he rose on his haunches to sniff for Runt and Bristle. He tried for them in all directions, but his nose was useless, the fine scenting nerves numbed by ash and soot. He barked for them, but the ringing in his ears was still the only sound he heard.

Pax worked his way out of the pile of brush and shook

off the debris. Soldiers streamed down the hill across the smoking patch of field and then plunged into the river. When they had passed, he followed. Each movement sent aftershocks through his bones.

Where he had last seen them, he called again for Runt and Bristle. There was no answer, but – faintly at first, as if they were reaching his ears from a great distance away – he heard his own barks. And then the sound of the wind, and the snapping of seared weed stalks as he crashed through them, and the rough shouts of the war-sick men as they returned to the trenches. And from the trees, a murder of crows, cawing their displeasure at the ruined world. Pax could hear again.

For an hour he paced the field, calling for the missing foxes. Dusk fell before he finally heard it: Bristle's weak answering yelp. He followed the call to the river's edge. There, the scrub oak was lying splintered and smoking over the bank, its blackened branches in the water.

Pax found Bristle tucked into the earthy ball of its roots. Her head was up and her eyes were alert, although her muzzle was matted with blood. The fur of her beautiful brush was burned to a black crust. Pax nosed her face. The blood on her cheeks was not hers.

She dropped her head. Curled beneath her was the still body of Runt.

Pax dipped his head to the little fox's chest. It rose and fell in ragged hitches, and Pax was relieved.

But then Bristle shifted and he saw: where Runt's hind leg should have been, where the neat black-furred leg and the quick white paw should have been, there was only a shredded red mess on the blood-soaked leaves.

*P*eter rubbed the chisel handle with oiled steel wool, trying to resist the urge to throw it across the barn.

The morning had been good. He'd crutched over field and woods, through mud and gravel, up hills and down rock faces, over stone walls and under fences. Strong, tireless, and nearly as fast as if he'd had both boots on the ground. At noon, he'd told Vola he felt ready to go now, and he was. But she had ignored him as usual. She'd ordered him into the barn to rest and taken his crutches hostage. "Foot up. Polish some tools. Get the hand feel of them."

His gaze fell on the near-finished carving in front of him on the workbench. The fox was rough, but it looked alive, and it seemed to him a sign that he would find Pax unharmed. Although it felt dangerous to hope, he allowed himself to imagine the scene. He would call for Pax at the spot where he'd left him, and Pax would come bursting out of the woods and probably knock him down in his happiness. They would go home together.

"You're going to polish that handle right off, boy."

Peter jumped. "I didn't hear you come in."

"You can't go drifting off when you're working with tools." Vola settled herself on a barrel beside him and picked up a rasp and an oily cloth.

"I was thinking about Pax." He put down the gleaming chisel and picked up his carving. He handed it over when Vola held out a palm.

"Looks like he wants to jump out of my hand. You're worried about him?"

Peter nodded. "But half the time I think he could be all right. Foxes are smart – really smart. We had to lock the door to the kitchen because Pax could open every cupboard. Once, he chewed through the wire to a fan we'd just put in my room. My father was really mad. But then, when he was trying to fix it, he found out the fan had a short in the housing. It would have caught fire. I think Pax knew that somehow, that he was protecting me. So why wouldn't he be smart enough to learn to hunt? Don't you think he could survive?"

"I do," Vola agreed.

Peter took the carving back and looked into the fox's face. "There's something else," he said. "It's that . . . I would know if he'd died." And then he told Vola what he'd never told anyone else – about the merging he felt sometimes with Pax, how sometimes he didn't just *know* what his fox was feeling but actually *felt* it himself. He held his breath, hearing how crazy it sounded.

Instead of laughing, Vola told him he was lucky. "You've experienced 'two but not two.'"

"That's on your board – 'Two but not two.' I didn't know what it meant."

"It's a Buddhist concept. Non-duality. It's about one-ness, about how things that seem to be separate are really connected to one another. There are no separations." Vola picked up his fox again. "This is not just a piece of wood. This is also the clouds that brought the rain that watered the tree, and the birds that nested in it and the squirrels that fed on its nuts. It is also the food my grandparents fed me that made me strong enough to cut the tree, and it's the steel in the axe I used. And it's how you know your fox, which allowed you to carve him yesterday. And it's the story you will tell your children when you give this to them. All these things are separate but also one, inseparable. Do you see?"

"Two but not two. Inseparable. So . . . a couple of nights ago, I was sure that Pax had eaten. I felt it. Last night, I saw the moon, and I knew Pax was seeing it right then, too. Do you think that if I *feel* Pax living, then he's alive?"

"Yes."

Peter's hopes swelled at her words. Vola never said anything she didn't mean. "We tell the truth here; that's the rule." She'd told him that about a hundred times.

It was a valuable thing, he suddenly realised, to have someone you could count on for honesty. How many times in his life had he wanted only that? How many questions had he needed an honest answer for and gotten instead, from his father, dark silence?

And then, before he could chicken out, he asked the one that haunted him.

"Do you think . . . Do you think if someone had a wild part, it could ever be tamed out? If it's in his nature? Inherited?"

Vola looked at him hard. Peter knew she thought he was asking about Pax, and he didn't correct her. He picked up the chisel again and looked down at it on his lap, his fingers squeezed white around the shank as he waited for the answer.

"You always been like this? Asking other people to figure out your stuff for you? *Eh?* That doesn't work."

Peter let out his breath. As soon as he'd asked the question, he'd realised he didn't want to hear the answer. Maybe he would never be ready to hear the answer to that question.

Vola patted her overall pocket and frowned. "Almost forgot." She pulled out a napkin-wrapped muffin and handed it to Peter. He'd eaten four of them at breakfast, but she was always convinced that he wasn't eating enough.

He unwrapped it. It was a little squashed, but as with the rest of them, the pecan was centred perfectly on the brown-sugar topping. She'd stayed up late last night baking them, and he had heard her singing something in a language he didn't recognise. Something happy. "Vola, why are you still living out here alone?"

"I told you."

"But twenty years to figure out who you are? I mean, how hard can it be?"

"Plenty hard. The plain truth can be the hardest thing to see when it's about yourself. If you don't want to know the truth, you'll do anything to disguise it."

Peter put the muffin down. She was avoiding his question. "But you do. You know yourself. So how come you don't go live somewhere with people? Tell me the truth. That's the rule around here, right?"

She looked out the barn window for a minute. Her shoulders slumped, and when she turned to him, she looked tired. "Fair enough, No-bat Peter. Maybe it's because I *do* know myself. Maybe what I know is that I don't belong with people. Maybe I am a grenade."

"What do you mean, a grenade?"

"What would you call someone who can go from a girl eating peaches and watching fireflies to a woman who kills a man? *Eh?* That girl would have cut off her arm before she'd have hurt a single one of those fireflies, but a few years later she killed a perfect stranger. I'd call that person

189

a weapon. I'm an unpredictable, deadly weapon. It's best I stay hidden here, where no one will ever be hurt by me, even by accident." She raised her fingers and popped them at him – boom! – but this time the gesture looked sad, not menacing.

"You don't hurt me," Peter answered.

"How do you know I won't?"

"Because I know." He thumped his chest. "In my core."

Vola slapped her palms on the workbench and pushed herself off. "Put those tools back in the right order," she muttered over her shoulder as she left.

From the window, Peter watched her stamp down the path. It seemed she was moving differently. As if that heart-pine leg of hers had grown even heavier.

One by one, Peter slid the cleaned tools into their pockets and then rolled the canvas. He felt his old anxiety coiling at the base of his skull. Over a week he'd been stuck here. He would've left already if it hadn't been for the third condition. He'd promised, and he owed it to Vola, but when he'd asked her at breakfast about building the stage, she'd only shrugged. "I'll get to it."

And then the solution hit him, so ridiculously simple that he laughed out loud.

Without his crutches he was awkward and slow again, but he managed to hop outside to where Vola kept a brush pile. There, he chose twelve long straight saplings, each the thickness of his arm. One by one, he flung them to the barn doorway, then followed and slid them inside. On the sawhorses, he stripped them of their branches, then set to work.

And two hours later, he had a stage. It wasn't much to look at – the corners raggedly notched and lashed with twine, mismatched scrap boards nailed on to the frame for the walls and floor – but when he strung a length of burlap over the top, he smiled. "Piece of cake," he said to François, who wandered in and stopped to sniff the frame in obvious admiration. "Piece of cake."

"I made the stage. It's in the barn."

Vola looked up from the chicken she was plucking. She eyed the branch Peter was leaning on and then motioned to his crutches, propped against the kitchen counter.

Peter reached for them, slid them under his arms, and felt the immediate comfort they brought. "I can do that puppet show for you now. Come to the barn."

"I have work to do now. But all right. Tonight."

"And then I can leave, Vola. I'm ready."

Vola laid the chicken on the table and sighed. "You are not ready. You sleep indoors, dry and warm. You have clean water, and someone cooks your food for you. But all right, tomorrow I will test you. Ten miles. You hike five miles, show me you can make a camp on one leg, and hike five miles back . . . then we'll talk."

Peter watched her gather up the chicken feathers and tuck them into a pouch. And it struck him: nothing would change after he left. Vola would save her feathers, would make her puppets all alone in the woods, more and more and more of them, and tell that soldier's story to no one.

21

Pax watched Runt all night and into the next day from a bush not far away. He left only to soothe his burned lip in the cool river mud and make a meal of the small fish he found lying on the bank. His sense of smell returned, and whenever he woke from a fitful doze, he sniffed for Bristle and Runt to reassure himself that they were still alive.

Bristle had dragged brush to the fallen tree to shelter her brother and curled her body over his to keep him warm. She left him briefly a few times, and when she did, Pax quietly took her place beside Runt's motionless form.

He was there when Runt finally woke with a whimper.

Pax nuzzled Runt's shoulder to comfort him. Runt lifted his head. His eyes were clouded with pain and fear. He cried out again, and Bristle, who had been hunting nearby, trotted back to him.

Pax pulled back, respectful, but Bristle merely settled herself alongside her brother, her cheek beside his. Pax bent to Runt's wound and licked it cautiously, wary of Bristle's reaction. She watched him carefully but did not object.

Pax set to a thorough cleaning of the wound. Runt watched him with a trusting gaze and did not flinch. When Pax finished, he cleaned Runt's face and ears. And Bristle allowed it.

When Runt had fallen asleep again, Pax stayed beside the two. Together, he and Bristle watched the activity of the camp.

Although the humans did not return to the ruined part of the field, the scents were dangerous. When the wind was from the west, carrying the smell of burned land, the men seemed tense. More arrived at the camp, with more machines. At the sudden growl of an engine, Bristle jumped. She laid her head back over her brother's. *I must move him soon.*

Humans cannot scent. If we are hidden from view, we are safe.

Bristle looked from him to the men. *We are not safe if a single human is nearby.*

Bristle seemed lessened to Pax, as if a vital piece of her had disappeared. He knew that somehow the humans had taken it. *My boy does not bring harm. He is not like them. He is not war-sick.*

The war-sick are full-grown. He is still young.

No. It is another difference. Pax was sure of this, but he was also confused. Over the past year, Peter had grown taller and stronger, and his voice had deepened. But more than that, his scent had changed — it was no longer the scent of a child. *He is not young. But he is not war-sick. The last day I saw him, he cared for me, although he himself was in pain. His eyes shed water.*

His eyes were wounded?

Pax thought for a moment about the mystery of crying. *No. When he is hurt in other places, his eyes shed water. It streams down his face. I think the pain is relieved by the flowing water. But his breath — he gulps for air, as though this pain-water may be drowning him.*

The vixen bent to lick more dried blood from her

sleeping brother's haunch. After a while, she raised her gaze to Pax, and in it, Pax saw the terrible things that had been done to her family by humans.

And then Pax understood something. Peter had thrown the toy into the woods that last day. The pain-water had been flowing from his eyes, but he had thrown the toy. And he had not followed.

My boy is not war-sick. But he has changed. He is now false-acting.

22

*P*eter lit the four big lanterns hanging from the barn rafters. The tools, the sharpening wheel, the wall full of puppets – all glowed warm and cheerful in the cones of amber light. Even the hay shone like Rumpelstiltskin's gold. The barn looked reborn but familiar. He knew it like a home now.

Home. As soon as he'd put on Vola's puppet show, just another hour from now, he would finally be free to start out again.

He lit the two small lanterns near the stage and lifted Sinbad from the wall. "Showtime." The marionette's black eyes looked back at him blankly. Peter checked the joints, still amazed that Vola had taken the puppet apart just so he could learn its secrets. And suddenly Vola's secret philosophy card flashed in his mind: "I would have been a good teacher."

She was right about that. He thought about how easily she suggested techniques in his drills without making a big deal of anything. How she had him watch while she carved, then let him figure out things for himself. How she asked him questions about everything and didn't answer for him.

But she was all wrong about being too dangerous to be near people. Anyone who knew her would tell her that.

The problem was that no one knew her.

Except maybe him.

He hung the marionette back on the wall. "I think, Sinbad, I'm going to give you the night off."

He went outside and fished a wrist-thick limb out of the brush pile. Back inside, he sawed off the ends and nailed on a base. He lashed the Roc's tin bowl nest to the top, then fixed it on the stage. Next, he lifted the sorceress puppet from its perch and unscrewed its left leg.

—«—

"Ready?" Vola called out.

Peter climbed the stack of hay bales he'd set up behind the stage and picked up the sorceress's controls, surprised his hands weren't shaking. Because suddenly, everything he'd been so sure of an hour ago now seemed like a terrible idea.

When she'd come into the barn, Vola had been wearing a long purple skirt instead of her overalls, and she had combed her hair, something Peter had never seen before. She had been astounded at the stage he'd built, and it hadn't been an act. "You have the makings of a woodworker," she'd said. "If I were in the market for an apprentice, I'd offer you the spot."

In another few minutes, what would she think of him? It was too late for second-guessing, though. "Ready," he lied.

Vola turned down the four overhead lanterns; then Peter heard her drag a stool to the middle of the barn.

"This is the story of a girl," he said.

He heard Vola take in a sharp breath. And then he didn't hear a sound after that.

Not when he pulled the curtain and drew the sorceress up from the plank, not when the seed corn he'd piled on her stomach like peaches spilled off. Not when he wrapped her in his camouflage T-shirt, tucked her hair into a clay-bowl helmet, and slid the stick into her hand as a rifle. Not when he had her shoot the rifle, not when he unscrewed her leg, not when he made her climb to the nest.

Peter had expected a protest when he lit the nest on fire, but still Vola didn't make a sound. And just as he'd practiced, the fire was only a momentary flare as the handful of wood shavings in the bowl flashed up. Just enough time for him to take off the marionette's army uniform.

He drew her up out of the nest and eased her to the stage, where he'd propped the child puppet beside his carved fox. He had her bend low to the child, then turn and stroke the fox. And then he pulled the curtain.

Peter hung the controls. He waited, but still there was only silence. He stretched to look over the stage.

Vola stared straight ahead, right through him, her face as rigid as if it had been carved of wood. The tears streaming down her cheeks gleamed in the flickering light. Somehow they only served to make her look noble.

"I'm sorry. I only meant . . . You're not a grenade. You're good. You took me in, you're training me so I can get Pax—"

"Leave me alone, boy." Her voice was low and wire tight.

"Wait. I think it's stupid to waste your life out here for some kind of punishment. I mean, maybe that guy didn't even care about that book. Maybe he won it in a poker game the night before. Maybe what he cared about was . . . I don't know" – Peter steeled himself – "being a teacher or something."

At the word "teacher," Vola shot her chin at him, but he didn't look away. "Yeah, maybe he wanted to be a teacher. So maybe you should go do *that* for him. But you'll never know, so I think you should go out and live *your* life. I'm just saying that whatever bad thing wrecked you before, you could start over like the phoenix and—"

"I know what you're saying. You're not wrong, but get out of here now. Leave me be."

Peter started to argue, but his words withered at the sight of her sitting so still, head so high, tears now rolling down her neck. He wrapped the sorceress's controls and then climbed down from the hay bales and picked up his crutches. The silence of the barn felt enormous. "Okay. Okay," he said, just to break it.

The walk to the cabin in the dark took forever. Inside, a covered plate rested on the counter. He slumped against the doorframe, washed in guilt. Vola had made it up for him from the dinner leftovers. "You pick this chicken clean later tonight, you hear me?"

A fresh wave of guilt. She'd killed a chicken, something she didn't do often, because she wanted him to have more protein.

Peter shoved off from the doorframe and scooped up a box of matches from beside the stove. He had no idea how long she'd stay out there, but when she came back, it wouldn't be to a cold, dark cabin. This much he could do for her. He lit all the lamps and then laid a fire just the way he'd seen Vola do it each night.

Sitting there, watching it catch and grow, he replayed everything he'd said. It had all been true. Well, the part about that soldier maybe wanting to be a teacher had probably pushed it, but who knew, maybe he had. No, there wasn't a single thing he hadn't meant to say. Nothing he regretted.

A gust blew down the chimney, threatening the fragile fire. He reached for another section of newspaper. As he crumpled it, a headline caught his eye. FORCES PREPARE TO ENGAGE. AREA TO BE EVACUATED.

He flattened the sheet and read. He studied the map, unbelieving.

And then he grabbed his crutches and pegged out to the porch so fast that François scrambled from his nest and shot out into the night. He jammed his clothes into his pack, then looked around. The phoenix bracelet, the photo of his mother, and his mitt and ball were the only things of his in the room. He propped the bracelet on the hammock where Vola would find it, dropped the other things into the pack, and swung up into the kitchen.

Vola was just coming in. She hung her hat on the peg and looked over to the fire, then back at him. At his pack.

He handed the sheet of newspaper to her.

Vola scanned it, then looked up for an explanation.

He pointed at the map. "The area they're closing off?" he choked. "That's only five miles from where I left Pax!"

"Are you sure? It's a big area . . ."

"I'm sure! See this empty place? It's an abandoned rope mill. It's got all these high stone walls, and it sits overlooking the river at the only place you can cross it — the rest is gorge. That's where they'll fight for the water. My friends and I used to play war at that mill. We said it was the perfect place for an ambush. We played *war*! I left Pax on the road leading up to it, thinking it would be . . ." The word "safe" stuck in his throat. He shot up and lurched over to the pegs at the door to grab his sweatshirt.

"Stop. They're preparing for battle there. Don't be crazy."

"It's not crazy. It's right. I know it now. Remember the cheese? You asked what kind I liked, and I didn't know? My father likes cheddar, so that's what we have. Maybe I used to like something else. It's like you said – I had that forgetting-who-you-are disorder. I didn't remember what was right and what was wrong when I left Pax. But now I do. Now I know I need to go there. I *know* that."

"All right. Maybe so. But you're still on one leg, boy. It isn't possible. Look at this distance." Vola sat down with the map.

"No! I've wasted enough time. I'm not listening any more."

"Hold on." Vola lifted the paper. "You come over here. See something."

Peter frowned, but he swung back over.

"Robert Johnson? Bus driver friend I've been telling you about, who's been mailing your letters? See this spot here?" She tapped the top left corner of the map in the article. "That town is the final stop on his route. He passes through here at ten past eleven Tuesdays and Saturdays, and this is where he pulls up at the end of the night. What if I put you on that bus tomorrow? Seems like that would save you at least two hundred fifty miles, leave you about forty to cover on your own. You listening now?"

Peter dropped his crutches and sank to the chair, jelly legged with relief. "You'd do that for me? Only forty miles – that's nothing!"

"No. Forty miles across woods and hills on crutches is not nothing. Three days at least, I'd figure, and it'll just about kill you. But I think you can do it. So you'll stay the night now? Deal?"

Peter took her hand and met her gaze. "Deal." Looking at Vola, her face still tear streaked from what had happened in the barn, he knew he couldn't leave things as broken as they were. And he didn't have much time to fix them. "Deal," he said again. "On three conditions."

23

The moon shone through the trees as full and creamy yellow as the eggs Pax had eaten a week before. His stomach cramped as he paced the river's edge.

Only three times in the week and a half since his humans had left him had he eaten a meal big enough to fill his belly, and the last one – a pile of fish rotting on the bank – he'd retched up minutes later. He had retrieved the cached ham and watched with pride as Bristle and Runt ate the meat, but he hadn't touched any of it. And he still had had no luck hunting. All his fat reserves were gone. His coat hung loose and he was burning muscle.

Pax trained his nose to the humans' camp, which, as always, tortured him with its rich food scents. Over the past two days more war-sick had arrived, and hundreds of them were massing to the south beyond. The ground vibrated with their threat. But Pax was hungry.

He looked over to where Bristle was guarding the sleeping Runt and signalled that he would leave.

Although he could see the camp directly above him, he chose his old route – up the gorge and across the ridge – because the guards on the wall were facing the river.

He padded up the rocks in the water, leaving no tracks. Away from the silence of the devastated field, his ears pricked toward the night sounds. He knew them now. They comforted him. The thin piping of bats, the careless crashing of a waddling skunk, the underground bustle of voles, the distant calls of owls – all these sounds told him he was not hunting alone.

Pax himself made no noise – he had learned the secrets of stealth from Grey and Bristle. Like a shadow, he slipped across the ridge, down the hill, and into the grub tent.

No easy meat hung this night, but the tables were piled high with vegetables and breads. He knocked a wheel of cheese to the ground. The taste was strong and strange, but he gulped until his belly stretched tight. As he headed back out carrying a hunk for Bristle, a familiar scent stopped him in his tracks. Peanut butter.

It was drifting out of a large metal can. Pax dropped the cheese. He stood to sniff at the rim. Like the rubbish bin at his boy's home, the can promised a variety of scraps. But above the commingled scents rose the one he craved more than any other. His whiskers ruffled in pleasure. He nudged the lid aside a few inches.

The clear jar lay on top of the heap, its sides still smeared thick with the creamy prize.

Pax edged his snout under the lid and bit the top of the

rim carefully. He knew from experience that this was how to grip the jar so it didn't cover his nose. He pushed away from the bin.

And the lid clattered to the stony ground, ringing an alarm in the quiet night.

Pax ducked under the table and froze, his pulse quickened.

Across the tent, the flap snapped open. A human stepped in and clicked on a beam of light. Even over the peanut butter, Pax recognised the scent: his boy's father.

Pax raised a paw, ready to dart in whatever direction seemed safest. The man swept the light around the tent.

When it fell on Pax's eyes, he winced but he didn't move.

His pupils adjusted, and Pax saw the man crouch to stare at him. Pax remained frozen, paw still raised, jar still clamped in his jaws, studying the man's face as the man studied his.

The man grunted, rubbing his chin. Then he gave a rough laugh. Pax lowered his paw an inch, holding the man's gaze, testing him. His boy's father laughed again, then rose and lifted the tent flap. He kicked his boot through the opening.

Pax knew the signal. The man had used it on him often at the door of the humans' house, at the door of his pen: *Go through,* it meant. *Go through right now and I won't harm you.* The pact was reliable. Pax sped past him into the safety of the night.

He didn't slow down until he reached the spine of the hill. He buried the jar and then crouched to watch for movement at the camp in the pre-dawn light. Although he was certain no humans had followed him, he took off east, snaking a loose loop for half an hour before doubling back to drop down to the river.

Runt was awake when Pax returned, and for the first time since the explosion, he was struggling to rise. Bristle urged him back down.

But Pax saw that his lips were cracked and his eyes

sunken. *He needs water.*

Bristle looked to the river's edge. A dozen full-bounds for a healthy fox – would it even be possible for Runt?

The little fox braced his forelegs. He tightened his haunches to rise, then looked back in surprise. The leg that had been part of him his whole life, as much a part of him as his own scent, was gone. He bent and sniffed at the wound. He looked up at Pax and then Bristle, as if searching for an explanation.

Again he strained upward. His one remaining back leg jacked him up, and Runt rolled on to his wounded haunch with a yelp of pain.

Pax leaped to stand by his injured side.

Runt got to his front legs once more and then straightened his one back leg. Again he canted over. This time, though, he fell against the strong tall flank of the older fox, and he did not cry out. He wobbled, searching for a new balance.

When he found it, Pax took a single step toward the water, then waited.

Runt stepped out. First, the two front legs. Then a dragging hop with the single back leg. And a collapse against Pax.

Again Pax took a single step. Again the small fox matched it. And again. And once more, until he didn't waver at all.

Bristle ran ahead to the bank. And step by wounded step, Runt closed the distance until he flopped down by the riverbank and stretched his neck out to lap at the cool water.

When he was sated, he dropped his head, his eyes closing. But Bristle nipped him. Soon it would be full daylight. He would be exposed. She ran upriver to a stand of cattails.

Runt limped after her. He was still clumsy and trembling and slow, but he did not fall once. Pax followed close by. Just as they reached the stand of reeds, Pax startled at the crackling of brush from downstream. Bristle's head snapped round, too, ears cocked to the same spot across the river. Something large was coming.

Runt dipped his head to sniff at a snail.

Pax and Bristle backed into the cattail reeds. Bristle called to her brother. Runt did not turn his head.

A buck pranced out of the vegetation, tossed his antlers, then splashed into the river.

Bristle barked for her brother again, and again he ignored her.

The deer clattered up on to the other bank, heading

for the bright grass of an unscorched area of field. At its edge, he lifted a hoof. As he set it down, the earth rocked and the bright grass blew. The buck burst up, his back twisting and snapping.

Runt screamed his terror at the quaking ground. Bristle and Pax herded him into the cool dark of the reeds and soothed him until he understood that he was unharmed.

The foxes watched the soldiers run down the hill, sweep their beams of light over the heap in the field, then go back. As a pink sun rose over the pines, vast patches of grass in the field flared up and crackled. Field mice stumbled out toward the cool safety of the riverbank. Dazed and disoriented, they would have made easy meals, but Bristle let them pass, as if obeying some code that protected those so terrified.

She stood and gazed over the smoking field. *We have to leave here. Now.*

Pax knew that she was right. He followed her out of the reeds. Bristle called to Runt, who was watching a wandering vole. He didn't even flick his ears toward his sister.

And Pax understood. *He can't hear.*

When *Peter came into the kitchen, he found Vola* already drinking coffee. She couldn't have slept any more than he had – he'd heard her leave for the barn in the middle of the night, and she hadn't come back until nearly dawn. She raised her mug. "Breakfast before you go?"

He shook his head.

Vola nodded and took his pack from him. She stuffed a brown paper bag into it. "Eat the ham sandwiches first – ham won't keep. There's a jar of salve – put it on twice a day. I filled your thermos, but you'll have to be on the lookout for springs. Keep that cast dry, though. I mean it. Tape a bin bag around it if it rains."

She set the pack down and Peter noticed – she had two shoes on. "Hey. You're wearing it."

She lifted her overall cuff. "Condition number one."

"Wow," Peter managed after a minute. "Holy *dyableman*. Where's the old one?"

Vola tipped her head to the armchair. "I don't know what to do with it. Maybe put it on the scarecrow?"

"Not on the scarecrow," Peter answered, instantly sure. He pointed to the fireplace. "The phoenix, remember? All his stuff burns in the nest."

Vola sighed, but she followed him. Peter stirred the embers and added some kindling. Vola brought the wooden post over. It looked smaller somehow. The leather straps reminded Peter of the ones binding the marionettes' feet and hands.

"You okay?"

"I'm okay." Vola placed the wooden leg on to the flames, and both of them watched until it caught.

Vola walked away first.

Peter noticed how smooth her gait was with the prosthesis. You wouldn't even guess. He pulled the screen over the fire. When she got home today, there'd be nothing but a pile of ashes. "You okay with the other two conditions?" he asked, trailing her to the kitchen.

"We'll find out at the library. But I loaded the tractor already."

"The tractor?"

"How else are we going to cart twenty marionettes into town?"

"We're driving to the library on a tractor?"

"We're driving to the library on a tractor. Unless you've got a magic carpet you haven't told me about. And we have to leave soon to make that bus, so . . . you're ready?"

"Yeah. I've got everything I need."

"Well, not quite you don't." She reached behind the door and drew out something that surprised Peter so much, he couldn't respond.

"You know what it is, right?"

The baseball bat was turned perfectly smooth, the weight so solid and balanced that the world seemed to slow as he hefted it. "You made this. But I don't need—"

"I think you do. Maybe when you get where you're going, you'll figure out why."

Peter ached to hand the bat back. But Vola had stayed up last night carving it for him, and she looked so proud. Maybe it was time to own one again. He balanced on his crutches and took a slow-motion swing.

And the other bad memory swept him.

His seven-year-old fury. A wildness he couldn't control. The exhilarating fright of that wildness. His mother's blue gazing globe, batted off its pedestal into a million shards. Her tears – "You've got to tame that temper. Don't be like him." Her bloodied fingers, picking the blue glass daggers from her white roses. His shame as he watched her drive away.

He slid the bat into his pack, where it fit as though it had always had a place there. Treacherous.

He hoisted the pack. Underneath was the newspaper clipping. He picked it up. And his eye caught the date.

He crumpled to the chair, gut kicked.

"What?"

"He knew." Peter shoved the clipping across the table. "He *knew*. This is twelve days old. So my father knew this when we left Pax." It hurt to take a breath, like knives to his lungs. "When I asked to leave Pax on that old mill road because it would be safe, he *knew*."

Peter's hands burned. He looked down. They were balled into tight fists. He forced them open. "How could he have done that?"

Vola came over, eyeing him carefully. "I'm sorry. That's a very bad thing."

His jaw clenched – could teeth shatter? He forced it open. "How could anyone have done that?"

"I know you're angry . . ."

Peter's fists had balled up again, the nails gouging his sore palms. He jammed them between his knees. "No. I told you. I don't get angry. I'm not like him. I won't be like him."

Vola sat down across from him. "Oh. I see. I see now. But I don't think that's going to work out. You're human, and humans feel anger."

"Not me. Too dangerous."

Vola threw back her head and barked her startling laugh. "Oh, let me tell you, feelings are *all* dangerous. Love, hope . . . Ha! Hope! You talk about dangerous, *eh*? No, you can't avoid any of them. We all own a beast called anger. It can serve us: many good things come of anger at bad things; many unjust things are made just. But first we all have to figure out how to civilise it."

Peter felt his wiring begin to snap. "Just one time, could you *not* tell me I have to figure something out? Just once, would it kill you to help? Come on, I'm leaving. You've got all this" – he waved his hand up to the bulletin board – "this wisdom. Would it kill you to send me off with some advice?"

"What, you want me to give you a philosophy bingo card for your trip? Like: When you smell honey in the woods, run because the bear can't be far behind."

"Yeah. I guess. But for real."

"Well, for real, I don't have any magic truth to guide you. It's your trip, not mine. But now that you bring it up, I do have a card for you." She pulled one off the board and handed it over.

"It's blank."

"It is now. But a trip like this? You will find something to fill it with. A truth of your own, that you discover on your own."

At that, Peter felt suddenly exhausted, as if he'd been holding himself rigid for years. He had been on his own for so long.

Vola studied him. "Oneness is always growing in the world, boy. Two but not two. It's always there, connecting its roots, humming. I can't be part of it – that's the price I pay for taking myself away. But you can be. You can vibrate with its heartbeat. You may be *on* your own. But you won't *be* alone."

"What if I get lost?"

"You will not get lost."

"I think maybe I already am."

Vola reached across the table, cupped his head, and pressed. "No. You are found." She got up, and Peter felt her brush a kiss on his hair as she passed.

The tractor wasn't actually that uncomfortable. But it was slow and bumpy and loud – too loud for them to talk easily, even though Peter was sitting right next to Vola. That was okay with him – he had a lot to think about. Even after they turned on to the smoother highway shoulder, Vola was quiet, and Peter figured she had things on her mind, too. But when she pointed at a hawk wheeling overhead, he remembered something he'd always wanted to ask.

"What is it with you and birds? The feathers?"

Vola patted the feathers on her rawhide necklace and smiled. "*Ti Poul*. When I was born, I reminded my parents of a bird. My hair stuck up like feathers, I had a scrawny neck, and I squawked for food all the time. I'm part Creole, part Italian, and part a dozen other things. But all people who revered birds in their cultures, my parents realised. So they named me Vola – it means 'fly' in Italian. But they called me *Ti Poul* – 'Little Chicken.'

"My chickens grace me with feathers, and I wear them to remember that when I was born, someone saw me as a bird. That's all, not much of a story."

But it was a good story, Peter thought. And it explained the look she always got on her face when she lifted the Roc. It would be the hardest for her to give away.

He looked behind him at the four crude pine crates the marionettes were packed in, strapped to the back. Peter hoped they didn't remind Vola of coffins. Her amazing puppets were going to live now. Really live, out in the real world, not just exist to perform as some kind of penance.

And maybe Vola would, too. But maybe that was too much to ask. He was still wondering about that when the tractor sputtered to a stop in the library parking lot, hunkering over three spaces.

Vola climbed down and hoisted one of the boxes. Peter followed her, but at the wide brick steps he stopped and tapped Vola's shoulder. "You know," he whispered, "you have to be a little careful in there . . ."

"Careful?"

"About . . . language. You know?"

Vola looked at him blankly. He was going to have to spell it out for her. "It isn't the kind of place where people say *dyableman* a lot."

"Oh, please. I think I know that, boy." Her tone was withering, but it held the hint of a grin. Peter opened the door and swept her through.

The librarian looked like a tossed handful of jewels: bright coral scarf, gold silk blouse, sapphire blue skirt. She smiled as Vola came in and set her crate on a table, and when the top was lifted, her mouth fell into a perfect O. Peter remembered he'd been speechless, too, the first time he'd seen those puppets. He backed out the door to give Vola some privacy.

The morning's clouds had lifted, and the sky was so bright that it hurt his eyes. The sounds seemed brighter than usual, too, or maybe it was just because things had been so quiet this past week. A barking dog, two women chatting, bike brakes squealing, children shrieking in a playground beside the parking lot – he had missed these

222

sounds. He had missed the world. He wondered if Vola missed it all the time.

He headed over to watch the little kids playing for a few minutes. Most of them were tearing around, jumping on to and off benches and slapping the swings in some kind of made-up game. A frowning girl with a straw-coloured ponytail was digging by herself in a sandpit, earnestly moving shovelful after shovelful from one pile to another. Sitting on the sandpit corner, looking bored, with his head propped in a baseball glove, was a boy in a faded red T-shirt.

The short-stop. From the ball practice.

Peter moved closer. "Hey."

The boy looked up, then stood, as if readying for a fight. He nodded at Peter's crutches. "I wondered why you didn't show."

"How did you do?"

The short-stop scoffed. "Like you don't know you creamed us." He took the little girl's shovel and handed her a pink sweatshirt. "Come on. Let's go home."

"Wait." Peter felt a crazy rising panic. Maybe being a hermit for a week had made him weird already. But the boy was lifting his sister out of the sandpit and they

223

were going to leave, and he couldn't let that happen yet. "Wait! You know when you're on the field and you know what you're supposed to do, and you're ready? When the game's about to start and the glove turns into part of your hand, and you know you're exactly where you should be? That feeling? Do you think that's peace?"

The boy scowled at Peter. He shook his head as if he wanted to shake off the whole encounter, and then started walking away, pulling his sister by the hand. Peter could only watch as they left the playground, feeling that something valuable had just slipped away.

At the gate, though, the short-stop turned. He was pretty far away, but it looked like maybe he wasn't frowning any more. He lifted a hand and shot two fingers up in a peace sign. Peter lifted his own fingers back.

Inside, the librarian was unpacking the last crate. Half a dozen kids had materialised, and they gaped and grinned as the she lifted out each marionette. Vola stood off to the side, watching. She turned to leave when she caught sight of Peter.

Peter stabbed out a crutch to block her. "Condition number three?" he asked with a glance back to the librarian.

Vola gave him a look that was half irritation, half grudging defeat. She turned back to the librarian. "I forgot to say, Bea, that I'll come back once a week. To teach the kids how to use them."

Bea Booker smiled – a slow smile that reminded Peter of melted caramel. "That'd be awfully nice."

Vola set out for the door, but Peter blocked her path again.

Vola threw her palms up. "What now?"

He raised two fingers.

"What? Oh, for . . . *Fine.*" She walked back to the table. "Bea. Twice a week. I'll come *twice* a week, teach the kids."

The librarian broke out into a wide grin. "The children would love that. Be good to see you more, too, Vola. Maybe we could go for that coffee afterward."

A little girl with a fountain of beaded pigtails tugged on Vola's overalls. She pointed to the elephant. "How do you make him dance?" she demanded.

Peter held his breath. But instead of lecturing the girl about figuring things out for herself, Vola crouched down to study the elephant. Peter noticed that the movement was smoother with the prosthesis. She had an ankle joint now – such a simple thing, to be able to flex. How much she had given up.

"What makes you think he wants to dance?" Vola asked.

"Red toenails, like mine." The little girl wiggled her toes in her sandals. Then her hand drifted up to stroke the feathers at Vola's neck.

Vola startled at the touch, and Peter held his breath again. But she only reached out and patted the girl's own necklace of yellow pop-beads.

Then she pointed to the clock over the desk, which read almost eleven. "I've got something important to do right now, but I'll be back in half an hour. If you're still here, we'll figure out how to make him dance."

By the time they grabbed Peter's pack and crossed the street, the bus was already idling at the station. While Vola went to the ticket counter, Peter made his way to the group waiting to board. A shiver of current scurried up his spine. It was the same thrill that juiced him every time an umpire called, "Play ball!"

Vola handed Peter the ticket. Lying in his hand, it looked too small for the power it contained. "I'm going to get there, and I'm going to find him. Thank you."

The bus door cranked open and Vola leaned in. She pointed a warning finger at the driver. "Robert, this boy is family. He's been visiting and now he's going home. You see that he gets there safe and sound."

She stepped away, and an elderly couple began their shaky climb aboard. Peter shifted his rucksack and crutches. He took a step toward the bus. Then he turned back. "I'm family?"

"That's as true a thing as I've ever known. Now get on that bus."

The steps were tall, but Peter hoisted himself up with ease. He took a seat up front and gave Vola a thumbs-up through the grimy glass. He was strong now. He was prepared. But when the air brakes hissed their release, he gripped the armrest. It was going to hurt a lot to watch her getting smaller and smaller.

Vola motioned for him to slide the window open when the bus growled into gear. "Boy," she called up as it lurched away from the curb, "I'm going to leave the porch door open!"

25

*P**ax dug.***

Since moving Runt up the gorge, Pax and Bristle had taken turns guarding him – a pact of protection. They would be his strong hind legs; they would be his ears. Runt was safe and sleeping inside the abandoned groundhog's den that Bristle had enlarged for him. Still, Pax felt anxious. Something was coming. He dug as he kept watch in front of the burrow. The pads of his paws were toughened. They did not bleed.

When Bristle returned from hunting, she dropped a chipmunk in front of him. Pax turned away, although he had not eaten since the cheese two nights before. He would not take food from Bristle or Runt.

Bristle buried the chipmunk and then stretched out beside the den for her watch.

Pax left to pace the perimeter of the clearing again. The location was good: although it was near the encampment, it was high enough above it to feel safe from the exploding earth down near the river. Juniper bushes ringing the clearing would provide cover. More important, they would help disguise the foxes' scents. A short distance away, a clear spring trickled from a cleft rock, and the grass was full of game.

But something was wrong. Something was coming. Pax bounded the short distance through the trees to the ridgeline above the encampment.

The encounter with his boy's father had left him too wary to attempt another raid. But at the same time he was more drawn to the camp. The man's motion – that sweeping kick of his boot through the doorway with its conflicting messages of goodwill and threat – had reminded him that he needed to protect his boy. And if the man lived at the camp, surely Peter would find his way there soon.

It was mid-afternoon. Pax watched the war-sick

spread out along the riverbank, rolling more wires, digging more holes, and burying more dark boxes under the hot sun. The odour of their sweat was spiked with a new aggression.

The danger he sensed was more immediate than that, though. It was more primitive. He ran back and paced the clearing again.

When he saw Runt emerge blinking from the den, Pax hurried over to examine him. No blood seeped from the wound, and it smelled clean. Runt ignored the meal Bristle dug up for him. Pax could see that he was thirsty. *I will take him to the spring.*

Bristle began to follow, but then she sat back down and merely watched intently as they left.

When they returned, Runt tumbled back into the den. Pax settled himself in front of it – the groundhog's burrow entrance felt too large, too open, and he felt better when he kept guard there – but Bristle called. *Come with me. Watch.*

She picked her way into the grass, paw over silent paw, head low and cocked to the ground. Pax followed as carefully. In the middle of the clearing she stopped short, ears perked forward, and shot a quick glance back at him.

Pax heard it. A light scurrying under the netting of

dried grass that matted the ground. Bristle tracked it as if she could see its movement. Then she sprang into the air and jacked straight down, paws over her nose, and emerged with a mouse in her jaws.

She ate it in a few bites and then angled back across the clearing, searching again. She dropped to her haunches, head cocked to her left. *Now you.*

Pax listened until he felt sure he had located the tunnelling rustle. A high leap, and then he tucked his paws over his nose to dive just as Bristle had. He landed hard. No mouse. He turned away from Bristle to huff out the dirt.

Bristle stalked off. Pax followed, his head hanging, until she perked her ears toward another faint scurrying.

Again she backed away while Pax tried the pounce. Again no mouse.

Bristle studied Pax as he pawed the dirt from his cheeks. *Follow me.*

Pax padded behind her until she stopped abruptly and dropped to a crouch. Before them was a hole in the thatch. It was warm with the fresh scent of many mice. Bristle warned him to stay back. *Don't move. Watch.*

Bristle crept forward. In front of the hole she dropped

and laid her head on her paws. She closed her eyes to slits, and her whole body relaxed, as if in deep sleep.

Pax was surprised – he had thought she was still teaching him to hunt. He stood. Bristle tapped a warning with her singed tail. *Stay.* Pax settled again.

For many moments, nothing happened. Then Pax caught the faintest stirring at the opening of the warren. A quivering nose tested the air, then retreated. Another long moment, and the mouse reappeared. Its movements were so light, so alert, that Pax knew it was a whisker away from flight. Bristle didn't stir, except for the flicker of an eyelid as she cut a warning glance at Pax.

The mouse emerged and retreated twice more. Then, assured that the fox was asleep, it made a run for cover. Bristle's swift paw swept out and raked the doomed mouse to her jaws.

Pax understood.

Bristle retreated to guard Runt, and Pax trotted into the clearing, eager to find the tell-tale hole that would allow him to try the move himself. He found one beside a rotting log and drew in the thick scents of a colony of field mice. He settled himself a foreleg's reach away.

His excitement made it hard to stay perfectly still, but

at last a mouse came to the entrance and tested the air. Like Bristle's quarry, the mouse darted back in at the sight of the fox. Like Bristle's quarry, it reemerged until it was convinced Pax was asleep and then made a run for it.

Pax wasn't as quick as Bristle. But he managed to knock the mouse over, and as it scrambled to its feet, he swiped again. And caught his first prey.

It was a small meal, but each bite sent a hot current through Pax's body. The mouse's life now merged with his own. His muscles brimmed with energy.

He sprang up and tore a joyful path around the clearing, running by Bristle in a blaze of red fur. She got to her feet to watch. Pax sped by again, scarcely skimming the ground, but it wasn't celebration enough.

In the centre of the clearing stood an old, crooked sweet-gum tree. Its lowest limbs reached out over a hollow; its upper branches glinted blue with feeding jays.

Pax flew at the trunk. He scrambled easily on to the first low branch and balanced there. Then step by cautious step, he began to walk along its length.

Leaves rustled around him in welcome like fragrant green stars. Through them, he looked down in astonishment. The world had changed. From this vantage point he could see through the ridgeline trees to the encampment and the river in the distance. The meadow grasses, which just a moment ago had brushed his shoulders, now seemed flattened to a broad green bowl. Jays flew down to scold him.

Pax recalled Runt's flight. He coiled himself. Then sprang, stretching out and out, feeling the air ruffle his belly fur. He landed lightly and threw his head back and barked his happiness.

This new world was his. He could travel through it, and he could feed himself on its bounty whenever he wanted. He was part of it all, free. But not alone.

Pax hurried to where he'd buried the peanut butter jar and unearthed it. He carried it back and dropped it in front of Bristle and Runt, who were drowsing at the burrow entrance in the last rays of afternoon sun.

Both of them came alive instantly at the strange scent. Bristle was on her feet first.

She nudged the jar and jumped back at its surprising roll. She sniffed it all around and tested it with her tongue. One taste was all it took. Bristle locked the jar between her paws and began lapping greedily, cleaning out the top half in seconds. She squirmed her snout in deeper.

Pax had done this same thing. *Be careful. You can get trapped.*

Too late. Bristle jumped up. She thrashed her head from side to side, but the jar was wedged on tightly. She hopped on to her hind legs, trying with both forepaws to claw it off, and tumbled over and over.

Runt watched in amazement. His sister had never lost her composure before.

Pax approached, offering to help. But Bristle dashed away. She would do this herself. Finally, she rolled on to her back and pried the jar off her face with her hind legs. She shook herself and stalked back, her head and tail high. She dropped down beside Pax and began cleaning herself.

Bristle had never sat this close to him before, with her flank pressed comfortably against his own. Her scent had never been this friendly. A streak of brown on Bristle's white cheek caught his attention. Without thinking of the consequences, he stretched out and licked it off.

And Bristle allowed it.

Pax cleaned her ears and her throat and her muzzle. And after a moment, Bristle returned the care. Cheek to cheek, the two foxes groomed each other. Bristle stopped to sniff Pax deeply. *You don't smell of humans now.*

Pax didn't respond. He got to his feet to test the air. Something dangerous had entered the clearing with the dusk. An animal scent he didn't recognise but feared. It was gone as quickly as it had appeared, but Pax howled at Runt.

Get inside the den. Now.

"K^{id!"} Peter twisted round so sharply, he nearly fell over. He'd been certain the guard station was empty – he'd watched for ten full minutes to make sure before leaving his cover.

A soldier came out from behind a truck. He lifted his rifle butt to the sign chained over the barricade. "No entry."

Peter straightened up as tall as he could on his crutches. It had been two days since he'd spoken to anyone. Two days since the bus driver had said, "I don't know what you're really up to, son, but I doubt it's a good idea. You want, I can get you on a bus back tonight. No shame in that," and Peter had replied, "No thanks," because there *would* have been shame in turning back, and then the bus driver had said, "All right then, good luck," and let him out.

Not a soul had spoken to him that night. The town was on the perimeter of the evacuated area, and the few people he passed cast their eyes down, picked up speed, as if they couldn't afford to make contact with anyone who might need help. *Nothing extra here,* their looks said. *All is already lost.*

The next day, from sunrise to well past sunset, and most of this morning, he had travelled on roads through vacant towns, past abandoned schools and playgrounds and neighbourhoods spookily silent without their squeaking tricycles, their car radios, their pick-up ball games. The only familiar sound had been water running through garden hoses when he'd filled his thermos.

He hadn't seen any other humans, but he'd seen the animals they'd left behind. A skittish pony, tugging up grass in front of a church. Dogs eyeing him balefully from behind Dumpsters. Dozens of skinny cats, sliding away,

their flanks hollow as spoons.

"Hey, kid!" The soldier moved closer. He eyed Peter's handmade crutches, the rough cast, the dirty clothes. "We evacuated this area almost two weeks ago. Where've you been, you don't know that?"

"I know that. But I left someone down there. I'm going to get him."

"Take it easy. We checked the records – everyone's out."

"He's not a person." Peter jutted his chin, defying the soldier to argue that this mattered.

Instead, the soldier's face changed, became somehow younger, and Peter saw that he wasn't that long out of high school. He slid his rifle back into its sling. "I have a dog. Henry." He didn't say anything else for a minute, just looked down the road, as if he were hoping this dog of his would suddenly appear. Then he turned back and sighed. "I don't think anyone's walking him. My sister said she'd do it, but she works. Want to see his picture?"

Even before Peter nodded, the soldier had drawn out his wallet. He held out a picture. A beagle. An ordinary beagle. Peter's throat hurt. The corners of the photo were worn soft and colourless. That picture had been taken out a lot.

"That's Henry. I got him for my eighth birthday. His hips are bad now, but he still likes his walk, you know? Still likes to sniff out squirrels and stuff. I told my sister that, but . . . Henry won't understand where I've gone, is the thing. He'll wait at the door all day for me. What's yours look like? I'll keep an eye out for him."

"Pax isn't a . . ." Peter stopped. If it didn't matter that Pax wasn't a human, why should it matter that he wasn't a dog? "He's red. Black legs."

"How big? Coyotes out here. They have pups this time of year. They'll take down a small dog when they have a litter to protect."

"He's pretty small." Peter shifted his weight off his blistered palms. "Please. I've come a long way to do this."

The soldier gazed at his photo another minute before slipping it into his wallet. When he looked back at Peter, he seemed older again. "We're holding them. But they're coming. You go in, you've got to be back out by tomorrow." He pointed at Peter's crutches. "You can do that?"

"I can. So . . . you'll let me through?"

The soldier looked around and leaned in. "This road is patrolled hourly, but we only guard the main trail entrances. No one is stationed in the woods yet. You travel twenty yards in, no one would stop you. But listen: if you get caught, I didn't just say that. Now get out of here."

"Thanks." Peter turned and started for the woods before the soldier could change his mind.

"Kid. I hope you find him."

It was quiet in the woods, but here the quiet was right, and it was broken by the sound of wild things, which seemed a promise. Here, Peter could imagine seeing Pax's red brush flicking between the trees. Here, when he called, it was easy to imagine an answering bark. These things raised his spirits so much that he could almost ignore the pain in his palms and in his armpits, bleeding and raw.

For an hour he pegged over ground that was so springy with decades of fallen pine needles, it seemed to lift him. When he heard the rough growl of a jeep, he ducked behind some brush until it passed. After that, he walked along the road's edge, sure that when another patrol went by, he'd have enough warning to take cover.

And then he was there.

It wasn't a landmark he recognised, or the way the road straightened out of its curve. It was the sense of betrayal that hung all around. He'd done something terrible here, and the place remembered.

"Pax!" he called, not caring if anyone heard him. Let the jeeps come, let a whole army come. He wasn't leaving without his fox. *"Pax!"* Against his shouts, the silence grew only deeper. Ominous now, not promising.

He started along the road again, calling and keeping his eyes to the gravel shoulder. He was sure Pax had had the toy soldier in his mouth when the car had peeled away. Whenever Pax had given up on Peter, he would have dropped it. Peter wanted to hold it in his hand again – a solid proof that his fox had been here.

He walked a quarter mile, a half mile, eyes down. And then he stopped short. He wasn't going to find that toy soldier. Because Pax *wouldn't* have given up. Not ever. Pax would never have thought he'd been abandoned – they were inseparable. Pax had known it all along. Peter was the one who'd had to learn it.

If Pax wasn't here, he must have gone home to find Peter, or tried – maybe the river would have blocked him, but maybe not. Dogs made it home against crazy odds all the time. Pax was ten times smarter than any dog, so why wouldn't he be able to find his way? Maybe he was there right now.

Home. Home was about ten miles southeast of the old

mill. And the mill was probably four or five miles south of where he was right now.

So he'd head south, calling for Pax all the way. The gorge beside the mill would be too dangerous to navigate in the dark, so he'd sleep there, then make the descent at dawn. He would cross the river where it widened out at the mill, and then after another ten miles of trails that he knew, he'd be home.

"Hold on," he said out loud. "I'm coming."

*P*ax woke with a start. *His boy was near.*

He jumped to his feet, waking Bristle, who had been dozing beside him, and began to search the clearing for Peter's scent.

Nothing. But he was near.

Pax bolted through the trees to the ridge above the encampment. He saw no youth among the war-sick. He did not hear Peter's voice among the murmurs and shouts. He crept down the hill and circled the camp as close as he dared, scenting from all directions. His boy was not there.

But he was near. And he was coming.

Pax returned to Bristle's side and lay down. But he did not sleep.

28

*P*eter travelled south for almost an hour, feeling certain
that Pax had travelled the same route. But when he
emerged from the woods, he stopped.

A vast meadow sloped down for at least a mile before
flattening into another mile of wide green floor. At the base
of that, the land rose hundreds of feet in jagged steps, as if
chopped with a giant hoe. And beyond that, rolling to the
horizon, was the forested plateau that hid the gorge.

Since waking, he'd travelled nine hours without
thinking of rest once, but now the stunning immensity of
the distance ahead drained what was left of his energy.

He dropped his pack and fell to the ground.

Nine hours of gripping the crutch handles had stiffened his hands to claws. He forced them open and felt the raw palms split. They'd blistered the day before, broken open, and blistered again. He poured cool water from his thermos over the hot pulp of his palms and set to work picking out shreds of tire rubber. Then he eased his extra pair of socks over his hands and looked out again.

A movement halfway down the valley caught his eye. Something trotted in bouncing dips between two trees. Fox movement. Peter rose to his knees. "Pax!"

There it was again. But no, whatever was there was tan, not red. Coyote, maybe.

The thought was a shot of adrenaline, and suddenly he was moving again, rucksack slamming against his back, crutches pistoning down the hill all the way to the valley bottom in just half an hour and then sinking into the boggier ground there, muddy and slower but still moving.

And then a ten-foot sheer rock wall loomed in front of him. The cliffs were a lot taller than they had appeared from across the valley.

Before he could second-guess himself, Peter hurled his pack and then his crutches up and heard them clatter on to a stony ledge. He wedged his fingers into a crevice and pulled. His cast scraped along the rough rock face, but his arms were strong from Vola's training, and he levered himself on to a shallow foothold. From there, he reached for a jutting tree, then another crack in the rock, and then he heaved himself over the first ledge.

It took an hour to climb the stepped rise that way: crutches and pack first and dragging himself after. When he reached the crest, panting and sweat-soaked, he fell to the ground under a tall pine. He drained his thermos in one swallow and ate the last of the ham sandwiches. He opened Vola's second packet.

Peanut butter. Peter's throat closed. He remembered the first time Pax had found an empty jar in the trash. He'd squeezed his snout in so deep, it had gotten stuck, and Peter had laughed until it hurt. He stuffed the sandwich back into the bag, wishing he'd found it the day before and tossed it to the dogs scavenging the Dumpsters, and got up again. It was almost six o'clock, and he had a way to go still.

As he travelled, the memories of those hungry-eyed animals accompanied him, darting and retreating like accusing ghosts. He wished he could tell them that he knew how it felt to have the one person who had loved you and taken care of you suddenly vanish. How the world suddenly seemed dangerous after that.

He had lost a parent. How many kids this week, he wondered, had woken up to find their worlds changed that way, their parents gone off to war, maybe never coming home? That was the worst, of course. But what about the smaller losses? How many kids missed their older brothers or sisters for months at a time? How many friends had had to say good-bye? How many kids went hungry? How many had had to move? How many pets had they had to leave behind to fend for themselves?

And why didn't anyone count those things? "People should tell the truth about what war costs," Vola had said. Weren't those things the costs of war, too?

With a start, Peter found that the dark was falling around him. A little panicked – he should have been looking for a good place to settle for the night – he spun round. His left crutch shot out on to a patch of loose stones. He fell on to it hard and heard a crisp snap. For an instant he feared *rib!* but the sound had been wood. He landed, still gripping the top of the crutch. Six feet away was its bottom shank.

"*Dyableman!*" It came out naturally, a satisfying word.

He tried out some other swears, and they felt pretty good, too. But the way the darkening woods absorbed his shouts without a response made him uneasy, so he stopped. He didn't have the luxury of venting, anyway. He had a crutch to repair and not much light left.

All around him, trees shot out hardwood limbs that he could tape to the broken pieces as a splint. But he had no hatchet to cut them. As he drew the bat out of his pack so he could find the tape, he realised that the solution was in his hand.

He aligned the crutch pieces, laid the bat over them, then began winding the tape. When he was finished, he tested the crutch with his full weight. It held, strong and solid. He wished he could tell Vola she'd been right: he had needed her bat on his journey.

He knelt by his pack again. The accident had been warning enough – he pulled out the things he needed to make camp for the night, then scraped a bowl in the dirt and filled it with a pile of twigs and dried grass. He touched a match to it, and a little fire crackled to life.

Peter held his jackknife over the flames until he figured it was sterilised, then gritted his teeth and slit open the new blisters that had formed on his palms. The pain made him gasp, but he eased on some of Vola's salve and took deep breaths until it numbed. The herb smell swept him back to her kitchen with a rush, and he wondered if she was there now. How was she managing without that heavy leg to anchor her?

Before he put his knife away, he held it up. The last of the firelight danced along its blade. He remembered the first time he'd seen Vola's knife, how shocked he'd been when she had gouged a chip of wood off her leg.

Peter tugged up his jeans. He pressed the flat of the knife against his calf and tried to imagine slicing off a nugget of flesh because it offended him, because it wasn't perfect.

A coyote howled then, and a second answered from a distance. Peter shivered. He turned the blade until the cool edge creased his flesh, then jerked it up. The slice was only half an inch, but its sting was fierce. There were advantages, he could see, to being made of wood.

The cut beaded up. As the dark blood began to drip, he drew it into the shape of a leaping fox. With his fingernail, he pricked out a pointed nose, then two ears. A wild smear of his thumb for the brush.

Pax. Tomorrow.

A red-fox blood vow.

29

*T*hree mice swelled Pax's belly and a muskrat dangled from his mouth, his first large prey. It would feed Bristle and Runt for the whole day. He craved sleep after a long night of hunting, but as usual he'd trotted a long weaving path home to confuse any possible predators. The trail the bleeding Runt had left when they'd moved was still strong enough to mark them as vulnerable.

The first rays of morning light lit the grasses. A movement caught his eye. Bristle. She was a few full-bounds out in the clearing instead of at the apron of the burrow, where she usually guarded Runt. He watched her bounce up in mock alarm and then tumble kicking into the grass. Then he saw an even more surprising sight: Runt's small head bobbed up.

Runt was outside. And he was playing.

Pax dropped the muskrat. He called to Bristle.

And Runt turned his head.

Pax called again, testing.

And Runt answered. He could hear.

Pax was washed with a relief so overwhelming that he could not move for a moment. Where he had once cared for only one boy, he now brimmed with love for this bristling vixen and her ragged brother. And they were safe.

He streaked across the clearing. Bristle and Runt parted to welcome him into the space between them. He dropped on to his back, and Runt toppled on to him. Pax rolled Runt over gently, listening for any whimper of pain, and heard only purrs of delight.

For an hour the foxes played. Runt rested often, and whenever he did, the other two stopped and flanked him. Like the buttercups beside them, their three fox faces lifted to the morning sun.

Until Bristle leaped to her feet, her nostrils flared.

Pax smelled it, too. The same threatening scent that

had made him anxious for two days. But this was no longer a faint thread in the air. This odour was strong and growing stronger.

Coyote! Bristle jumped toward the den, pivoted toward the clearing, then jumped back to Runt. Pax had never seen her so panicked.

At that instant, all three foxes perked their ears sharply to the same spot in the woods. To the careless branch rustling of a creature that did not need the advantage of stealth. Heading north, up from the gorge. Heading for the clearing.

The coyote was following Runt's trail.

Bristle nosed her brother upright and screamed at Pax, *Guard him!*

Pax herded Runt back into the den. Pacing the entrance, he watched Bristle head toward the rustling, stiff-legged and wary, and then stop. She pricked her ears, her rump high.

And then in front of her, at the precise place where the junipers were still compressed from dragging Runt in, a dark brindle coyote emerged, his head to the ground.

Bristle barked. The coyote's head snapped up. Bristle barked again and jumped into the clearing.

The coyote cocked his head and took a step toward

her. Then he lowered his nose to Runt's trail again.

Deep instinct urged Pax to run away. The coyote was a tall, heavily muscled male. A fox was no match for an animal that large and aggressive. But a deeper instinct reminded him that Runt was defenceless in the burrow.

Bristle ignored the instinct to flee as well. Instead, she tore straight toward the coyote, lunging at his flank.

The coyote spun and snapped, just clipping Bristle's back foot. She limped into the clearing, whining as if she'd been injured. The coyote studied her but then he shook himself, recognising the ploy, and dropped to the scent again.

Bristle flew back. She jumped in front of the coyote's path and faced him, her spine arched. From her throat came a hoarse howl Pax had never heard before.

For an instant, the coyote pulled back, seeming surprised that the small fox was engaging him. Then he bunched his shoulders into attack position and bared his teeth.

Pax's body stiffened. A growl rattled in his throat. Runt whimpered in the den.

The coyote sprang at Bristle and knocked her to the ground. For a moment, Pax saw nothing but fur and teeth flashing in the grass and heard only yips and growls. But then Bristle scrambled out of the coyote's hold. She leaped again toward the centre of the clearing. A single leap only.

Pax understood that she was luring him away from Runt. Staying just out of his reach, she baited the coyote until she reached the sweet-gum tree.

Then, just as Pax had done, she leaped up on to the slant of the trunk. She padded out on to the low first branch carefully, never taking her eyes off the growling coyote who followed on the ground. When she reached the spot where the branch split, she was well over his head. She hissed a taunt.

The coyote jumped. He clawed only bark and leaves. He circled in the hollow under the branch, looking for higher ground, and then jumped again. This time his forepaws caught the branch and held for an instant before he fell back. He gathered himself and leaped again.

Pax saw that Bristle was as far out on the limb as she could go. The coyote would tear her from the tree soon, or grow impatient with her distractions and return to the trail she'd diverted him from. She would follow and fight until he ripped her apart.

Stay! Pax ordered Runt. And he tore across the clearing.

30

*P*eter stared.

There'd been a birch tree by the upper walls of the mill. He and his friends had named it the Pirate Tree because in the fall, bright yellow leaves made it look covered in gold coins. He'd tied Pax to its trunk once when the kit hadn't liked their war play. The Pirate Tree was still standing, but now only blackened wisps tattered its branches. Nothing else, except the mill itself, was recognisable.

All the trees in the lower field were gone, uprooted and blasted to splintered logs. Great patches of grasses around them were scorched to ash. The bank was littered with the crow-picked remains of perch and crayfish and turtles and frogs.

What hurt most to look at was the water. The last time he'd been here, he'd dived into the pool at the base of the gorge. The water had been so sparkling and clear that he'd been able to see the pale green shafts of the reeds, the iridescent scales on the trout, and even, when he looked up, the sheer blue nets of dragonfly wings skimming the surface. He might have been swimming through liquid diamonds.

Now muddy boulders clogged the river, and the pool was a dull brown ring. The broad flat of the river was half its usual breadth. Mud flats near the banks, caking to dry clay, smelled of death.

The water was what the whole war was about. Peter remembered Vola asking him which side his father was fighting on.

Peter had answered her, stunned that she would even have to ask. "The *right* side," he'd added, indignantly.

"Boy," Vola had said, and then "Boy!" again, to make sure she had his attention. "Do you think anyone in the history of this world ever set out to fight for the *wrong* side?"

The wind picked up and howled across the field, stirring eddies of ash. Peter tried to imagine playing here again. It would be a long time before anyone would ever want to play here.

Vultures, wheeling silently above him, were the only living things as far as he could see. With this much devastation, they must have been feasting for days. He watched them, paralysed by the sadness of the scene. The closest two were circling a hemlock bough near the bank, probably judging the safety of returning to the meal he had interrupted.

A meal that might be . . . Peter couldn't form the thought, but he couldn't erase it, either. If Pax had been here, he could be dead now. And if he was, the vultures would lead him to the proof.

They hovered over three distinct spots – the one beside him and two across the river – slow and lazy. In no hurry. Their meals weren't going anywhere.

He dropped his pack. Freed of the weight, he swung down to the hemlock bough in only a few steps. Trailing from beneath it was the sight he was dreading. A fox tail, its white-tipped brush unmistakable. He lifted the limb.

The fox carcass had been scavenged, but its pelt

remained. And it wasn't red. It wasn't red.

Not Pax.

He took a ragged breath. Dizzy with relief, he pegged down to the river and waded in. When he was waist high, the crutches skidded out on the mud-slimed stones, so he speared them over to the far bank and dived in. For the first time in almost two weeks, Peter didn't feel hampered by his broken foot. He swam strongly.

He pulled himself on to the bank. Out of water, the soaked cast felt like it weighed a hundred pounds, the muddy plaster already crumbling. He took his knife out of his pocket and hacked at it until he freed his foot. It hung pale and limp, but the swelling was down and the bruise was almost gone.

Peter crawled to his crutches and hitched them under his arms. Upright, he saw what the larger group of vultures was circling: the corpse of a deer. He thought of the doe he'd seen in Vola's field – *You humans. You ruin everything* – and turned away from the sight.

Twenty yards up the field, a single vulture hovered over the third spot he'd sighted. Peter climbed, choosing a path where the grasses had been burned – easier going.

At first there seemed to be nothing on the charred

ground. But when he was almost upon it, he saw. A hind leg. Fleshless and singed, but still he knew it was a hind leg. A slim, black-furred hind leg with a small white paw. A ragged drift of fur at the top was bright cinnamon.

Fox.

Peter swayed on his crutches. Maybe it wasn't Pax's. Wasn't it too small to be Pax's? He wished he could know, and then he took back the wish. What did it matter, anyway? A fox had been going about its life here, and some humans had obliterated that life – wasn't that enough of an outrage?

He would scrape the earth with his bare hands and bury the remains.

Peter dropped to the ground. He swept a circle bare of rubble. And his hand brushed something that turned the breath in his lungs to ash.

A toy soldier, sighting down the barrel of a rifle pressed tight to its hard green cheek, aiming at whatever happened to be in the way.

Peter keeled over. *"PAX!"*

31

*P*ax reached the tree just as the coyote sprang again, this time finding enough purchase to hang from the branch. Pax flew at him and bit a mouthful of brindled fur and hung on.

The coyote dropped and sank his teeth into Pax's shoulder, all in one motion. Pax jerked free and then backed toward the south edge of the clearing, hoping to lead the coyote away from the tree, away from the den, away from the foxes he loved.

The coyote didn't follow. He threw back his head and

barked. Then he turned to eye Bristle again.

Pax lowered himself and began to creep back toward the tree. But then he stopped. He swung his head toward a sound from the encampment.

His boy's voice?

Ahead, the tall coyote barked again, and this time the call was answered. Three sets of ears cocked at the same spot in the juniper ring. A second coyote trotted out. Another male, this one pale and stocky. He surveyed the scene and broke into a gallop for the tree.

Bristle issued another threat yowl and spiked her fur, but Pax saw her eyes roll in terror.

The second coyote pawed at the trunk.

And then Pax heard it again. His boy, calling his name.

He bolted out of the clearing and through the stand of trees. At the ridgeline above the mill, he stopped.

War-sick men streamed from the walls, sticks raised, converging on a figure down on the field.

It was a black-haired youth, curled on the burned ground. His boy? The wind, blowing from the north, told him nothing.

The soldiers stopped, their sticks still menacing. The boy rose. He was tall, but Pax saw that his body didn't look like Peter's – this boy's shoulders were thrown wide, and braced under one was a narrow pole. Stranger still, this boy held his head high, not canted downward. He faced the men in defiance, something Pax had never seen Peter do, and raised his fist and shook it at them.

A single soldier ran down to the field. This one moved like his boy's father. He shouted, and the voice was familiar. But then the man walked to the boy and embraced him, something Pax had never seen the father do.

Were these his humans? Pax tried to scent, but the gusting breeze carried only the musk of enraged coyotes. He turned back for the clearing.

32

*P*eter let his father hug him. *For so many years he had
wanted to be in that circle of protective love.* He
felt his father quake with sobs, and he wanted to reassure
him that everything was all right. But it wasn't. His hands
stayed clenched – one on the crutch grip, one on the
toy soldier.

He pulled away. "What are you doing here? You told
me you would only be laying wire . . ."

And then he understood everything at once. Why the
men hadn't advanced. How the grasses had been burned
and the trees uprooted and the river strangled with rocks.

How there could be nothing left of a fox but a single leg.

"You knew." He shoved the toy soldier into his pocket and picked up the fox leg. "You knew! And you did this! *Pax!*"

33

*A*gain Pax *thought he heard his boy's voice. He* pricked his ears back to the camp.

Just then, the wind shifted. Pax smelled the war-sick's sweat, their cordite, their motor fuel, their charred fields.

And his two humans.

He ran back to the ridge.

He saw his boy lift something from the ground. A stick, but not a stick. Something furred and broken.

The grief-yearning scent rolled up the hill. Fresh and keen, from his boy. But also old and strained, from his boy's father. So this scent was not Peter's alone. It was the scent of humans.

His boy held the broken thing above his head and cried something angry. And then, "Pax!"

And Pax barked.

34

*P*eter held what was left of the fox high above his head and called his name again. "Pax!"

And from above the mill, an answering bark. Hope rose in his throat. But no, he must have just wished for that bark.

He scanned the ridgeline anyway. A flash of red. A white-tipped brush. A fox appeared in an open spot and rose on his back legs – on two back legs? – and looked straight at him.

Peter pressed the fox leg into his father's hand. "Bury this." Then he grabbed his other crutch and turned for the hill.

"Wait, Peter! You have to understand. It's my duty."

Peter pointed to the fox on the ridge. He thumped his chest so hard, it hurt. "That's mine."

His father shouted to him about wires; he shouted at him to stop. Peter saw the wires; he poled over them. But he did not stop. Because there was only his fox, waiting on the spine of the hill, and the distance between them. Over and over, he planted his crutches and swung through, closing that distance.

When he was almost there, his shirt dried from the wind and then soaked again in sweat, he stopped and called. Pax tossed his head and then bounded away toward the trees.

On four legs! Peter was sure of it: Pax was unharmed.

Peter followed. But again, just as he neared him, Pax broke away, galloping into the trees.

Peter followed again. He didn't begrudge Pax this testing game. He had broken his pet's trust – why wouldn't he be skittish? Why wouldn't he need to assure himself of Peter's loyalty now? For as long as Pax wanted, Peter would obey – it was fair punishment. Through the trees, a hundred long yards and a hundred more, Peter followed.

And then they broke into a clearing, and the fox stood and waited. Peter reached him. He offered his hand. "I'm sorry. I'm so sorry . . ."

Pax locked Peter's gaze and then took his wrist in his jaws. Peter's pulse jumped against the bracelet of teeth, pressed just tight enough to claim him. Just tight enough to call to Peter's own wildness. Two but not two.

Pax released Peter's wrist and tore across the clearing toward a crooked tree. Circling the tree was a pair of coyotes. Pax lunged at the taller one.

"No, Pax! Come back!" The tree was so far away – fifty yards at least. Peter dug his crutches into the turf and piked hard.

When he was a dozen yards away, he saw the coyotes' treed quarry – another fox, bright furred with a sharp and delicate face – a vixen. She was bleeding from a gash on her haunch, and instead of a thick brush, she thrashed the blackened whip of her tail.

The vixen swiped at one of the coyotes from above, taunting him, and Pax snapped at the other's flank. Peter saw that the two foxes were a team.

And that they were no match for the coyotes.

Peter barreled for the tree, shouting, but the coyotes ignored him. The taller of the two spun round and sank his teeth into Pax's neck. Pax shrieked.

And Peter roared in fury. He braced himself on one crutch and leaned back and side-armed the other, heavy with its white ash bat, as hard as he could, aiming in between the two coyotes.

Both of them wheeled round at the outrage. While the tree rang with the bat's blow, the tall dark one sprinted away and disappeared into the brush. The other one bolted a dozen yards and then stopped and turned back.

He eyed Peter and bared his fangs.

Peter bared his teeth back. Pax growled at his side, hackles raised, ready to spring. Peter swept his second crutch over his head and roared again, and Pax snarled and the pale coyote reared back in surprise. He turned and crashed out of the clearing.

Peter clutched the tree. He slid to the ground, shaking.

Instantly Pax was on him, wriggling under his neck, licking his face, sniffing his broken foot, nuzzling his face again. Peter wrapped his arms around his fox and pressed his face to the piney-smelling fur. "You're okay, you're okay, you're okay!"

The vixen leaped over them to the ground and disappeared into the juniper scrub ringing the clearing. Pax sat up and barked to her from Peter's lap.

After a moment, Peter saw a black muzzle point out from the brush.

Out came a skinny fox, about the size Pax had been at

eight months, blinking in the sunlight. He stumbled into the clearing on three legs. The vixen re-emerged. She paced and yipped at the runty little fox, shooting wary looks at Peter.

Pax squirmed out of Peter's arms and barked again. The three-legged fox took a few steps closer. Its limp was so awkward, Peter realised he must have lost the leg only recently. And then he made the connection.

He offered his hand and called softly. Hesitatingly, his gaze darting between Peter and Pax, the little fox hobbled over. He tucked his head under Pax's chin.

Peter extended a finger. The injured fox allowed him to brush his neck for an instant, then hurried back to the safety of the vixen's side.

Together, the two foxes looked expectantly at Pax, and then they melted into the underbrush.

And Peter understood. His fox belonged to them. And they belonged to Pax. Inseparable.

All this way he'd come. All this way.

Peter got to his knees. He placed his hand on Pax's back and felt the muscles jump.

Peter looked around. The woods looked dangerous now, full of coyotes and bears and, soon, humans at war. He looked down at his fox, still straining to follow his new family. "Go. It's okay." It wasn't, though. The pain scoured him hollow, left him without breath, like a kick to the heart. He pulled his hand away, because Pax would feel a pain that deep and he wouldn't leave. "Go!"

Pax shot away toward the brush line. Then he turned back to look at his boy.

Peter felt tears roll down his face, but he didn't wipe them away.

Pax sprang back. He whimpered, licking at the tears.

Peter pushed him down. He found the crutch and levered himself upright. "No. I don't want you to stay. I'll always leave the porch door open, but you have to go."

Pax looked toward the brush and then back at his boy's face.

Peter dug into his pocket and pulled out the toy. He lifted it.

Pax raised his head, his eyes trained on Peter's hand.

And Peter hurled the plastic soldier over the brush and into the woods, as far away as he could.

Sometimes the apple
rolls very far
from the tree.

ACKNOWLEDGMENTS

———⟨⟨⟨———

Red foxes. The more I learned about them, the more I admired them and the more determined I became to portray them with respect. I am indebted to Matthew Walter, a New York State biologist and skilled wildlife tracker who has spent years researching red foxes in the field. Where the fox behaviour is accurate, it's because he generously shared his expertise. Where it's not, I've made a choice to serve the needs of the story. I urge readers to do their own research about this splendid animal.

Without the following people, *Pax* would still be a roomful of crumpled pages: My kids, who, although grown, continue to remind me of the extraordinary bonds possible between children and animals. My writing groups, north and south— smart, insightful writers who don't tolerate lazy sentences. My agent, Steven Malk, who understood and loved this book from the day I shared its tiny seed. My editor, Donna Bray, for her brilliant guidance. All of HarperCollins for the incredible support. Patient David, for all the times I was with the foxes.

And finally, Chris Crutcher—thank you for the story behind the story within the story. You know the one.

PENGUIN BOOKS

Please return/renew this item by the last date shown.
Items may also be renewed by the internet*

https://library.eastriding.gov.uk

Please note a PIN will be required to access this service
s can be obtained from your library

ABOUT THE AUTHOR

Daniel Silva is the number one *New York Times* bestselling author of *The Unlikely Spy*, *The Mark of the Assassin*, *The Marching Season*, *The Kill Artist*, *The English Assassin*, *The Confessor*, *A Death in Vienna*, *Prince of Fire*, *The Messenger*, *The Secret Servant*, *Moscow Rules*, *The Defector* and *The Rembrandt Affair*. He is married to NBC *News Today* correspondent Jamie Gangel. They have two children, Lily and Nicholas. In 2009 Silva was appointed to the United States Holocaust Memorial Museum Council.

If you would like to find out more about Daniel Silva and his novels, visit his website: www.danielsilvabooks.com